Grig

JESUS' CAT

Stories

PUBLISHED WITH THE SUPPORT
OF THE MINISTRY OF CULTURE OF THE REPUBLIC OF ARMENIA UNDER
THE "ARMENIAN LITERATURE IN TRANSLATION" PROGRAM

JESUS' CAT

STORIES

by Grig

This book was published with the support
of the Ministry of Culture of the Republic of Armenia under
the "Armenian Literature in Translation" Program

Translated from the Armenian by Nazareth Seferian

Proofread by Teresa Wigglesworth-Baker

Book cover and layout interior created by Max Mendor

Publishers Maxim Hodak & Max Mendor

www.glagoslav.com

ISBN: 978-1-912894-36-9

A catalogue record for this book is available from the British Library.

GRIG

JESUS' CAT

STORIES

Translated from the Armenian by Nazareth Seferian

GLAGOSLAV PUBLICATIONS

Contents

FOR THE "LITTLE GUY"

A *human being* has entered the world of literature; he knocked softly on the door, walked in with his stories in his hands, and is standing there, waiting.

There is a reason why the word "human" was emphasized in the beginning. One of the most talented writers of the young generation, Grig, has entered the world of literature looking for human beings, to understand and to get to know them better and to avoid hating them despite knowing them, and instead to learn to love them. He has come to support human beings in their most difficult of tests, their gravest of missions – to live. Who else would agree to take on such a burden? Who else would be ready to support "the little guy" if not the Human Being? From the very beginning, Grig has stuck his "ladle" so deep into the twisted broth of the human soul, into its tangles and paradoxes, that you can't help but be afraid – will he have the strength to pull it out, extract it from there and see what comes out? Will he be scared by what he sees, will he manage to bear it? I'm convinced that he will manage, because he has set about his task with talent and patient diligence, because he loves human beings and literature; the twenty stories brought together in his first book, *Jesus' Cat*, bear witness to that.

Globalization, standardization, noisy ups-and-downs, barbarity, emptiness, political and religious conflicts, wars… How many "little guys" are squished both spiritually and physically under the powerful quakes of all these things? It is easy to love your nation, your people, the whole of humanity, but it is extremely difficult to simply and truly love one person, one individual. Today, literature is unfortunately also being swallowed by Big Business and Politics, serving their whims and interests, and taking writers with it too, subjecting them to the same, standardizing them, and it is only the rare brave soul that maintains an independent view, and continues to fight for mankind's genuine freedom, justice, true love and faith, for the sake of real literature. Grig is one of the brave souls. Grig has something to say. He says it through these wonderful stories today; I have no doubt that he will also say it through novellas and novels tomorrow.

Gurgen Khanjyan

JESUS' CAT

THE LITTLE GUY

The first time I met the Little Guy was on the fifth of November. It was a humid day, the leaves had already fallen and mixed with the mud, making the ground slippery. I left the university and decided to walk to the Vernissage to buy a book (I would often buy books there; they were cheaper than in bookshops). I was lost in thought and walking unhurriedly, I had almost reached the Vernissage when I saw three or four small paintings placed at a slight distance from the sidewalk, lined up under the trees. I walked up and took a look – they were all paintings of clouds. They were primitive, commonplace paintings, even bad works of art to some extent, but there was something in those clouds that pulled me toward them. I stood there looking when a short man, not particularly well-dressed, greeted me politely and asked me whether I was considering buying a painting. He caught me off guard, I thought he was just another homeless person who was about to beg for money, but he turned out to be the artist who had painted those pieces.

"Is this your work?" I asked.

"Yes, that's mine," the Little Guy said in an off-hand way and, walking up to the paintings, he used his foot to brush aside a few leaves that had landed in front of them. I cast another glance at the man and looked him over more carefully, as if to verify what he had just said. He was a short man past fifty, his clothing and hands had been smudged with paint in various spots.

"What's your price?" I asked just for the fun of it; I knew I wouldn't be able to buy anything because all I had was two thousand drams and a few coins.

"I'll let you have it for twenty thousand," the Little Guy replied.

"Um… will you be here tomorrow?" I asked, giving my voice a tinge of palpable regret, "I don't have much money on me right now."

"Yes, I'll be here," he replied slightly sorrowfully, "But, if you want, you can pick the one you like now, and then you can bring the money tomorrow, or any other day."

I was surprised by how educated and proper his words came out, so I tried to sound as educated as I could.

"No, I'll definitely come by tomorrow," I replied with a smile, but I knew that it was impossible for me to make twenty thousand drams in a single day. The Little Guy walked up silently to the paintings and moved them around, then he walked a slight distance away to a rock, where he sat down and started to smoke. I cast another look at the paintings and continued to walk. Naturally, I did not keep my promise; I did not go back to buy a painting, and I had forgotten the Little Guy, until he reminded me himself.

It was a surprisingly sunny day, although cold, and I was walking home from class, when I stuck to my habit of picking a longer route, so that I could walk through the small park (there's a small park, more like a garden, between the buildings on Komitas Street; I'd made a habit of walking through it). When I got closer to the park, I noticed that the Little Guy was standing there. I thought that he wouldn't remember me and decided to walk past him so that I could take another look at the paintings. They were familiar pieces, familiar clouds, and I walked rapidly past after throwing them a quick glance. I had almost walked past him too but, to my surprise, the Little Guy said hello. He caught me off guard to such an extent that I felt like I had been stripped naked and put on display in front of a crowd. My embarrassment was multiplied further when he said nothing about buying a painting after I had greeted him in return; he had simply said hello to me with no ulterior motives.

"I'll be right back," I said after an awkward silence, "Don't go anywhere, all right?"

I rushed home. I had decided to fulfil my promise no matter what the price. The situation in which I had ended up was killing me. His behavior had forced me to see how low I had stooped, it was unbearable. I wouldn't have felt that bad if he had reminded me about buying his painting, but his silence had been too much. The ten thousand dram note my grandmother had given me on my birthday was still there in my cupboard. I decided to give him that money now, and to pay off the rest later. And that's what I did. The Little Guy did not object. He took the money and asked me which painting I wanted.

"Why? Aren't they all the same?" I laughed and walked up to the paintings.

"What?" he was taken aback, "Can't you see? These are the clouds of a sad man, these are the ones of a hungry person…"

He gave similar absurd descriptions to each of his pieces, even though all the paintings had the same clouds on them – commonplace clouds that one can see in the summer sky, pure and bright.

"I don't understand," I said, smiling. "There are clear and bright clouds painted on each of these pieces, but you've given them sad names. I mean, if they were darker clouds, like the ones we have in the sky today, I would have agreed with you."

"But the clouds today are happy ones," the Little Guy looked up at the gloomy, gray sky and smiled.

It was only then I noticed that the man's front tooth was missing.

"All right. I'll take the 'lonely man's cloud,'" I said laughing, "But I can't remember which one it is."

He gave me the painting and we agreed that I would pay him the other half of the sum in small installments. When I asked for his phone number, he said I wouldn't need it, that he would be in the park from then on because it was located conveniently and there was a lot of foot traffic through it. I went home, my conscience at peace. Although I did not like the painting very much, I could stare at it for hours, the clouds seemed to be on the verge of moving at any moment. I turned the painting around this way and that, hoping that I would spot his signature somewhere, but in vain. I did not hang it on a wall, I didn't want my family to see it. I knew they would admonish me for buying it. Every day before I left for university, my mother would give me a thousand drams and a few coins, sometimes more. And, every day, I would give that thousand dram note to the Little Guy; I wanted to be relieved of my debt as soon as possible, even though he did not hurry me, as if it were all the same to him whether I not I paid off what I owed. That was how my friendship with the Little Guy began. I would often stand next to him and we would talk about various things; I would do most of the talking. I had noticed that he was the kind of person whose words seemed simple and insignificant at first, but would then mature within you over time and give you food for thought. One day, when we were talking about something I cannot recall at this point, I asked him whether he believed in God.

"I'm an atheist by God's own will," he replied.

"I don't believe in the existence of God," he said when I asked him to explain this strange statement, "But I do believe that God has willed me to be an atheist."

Our conversations went on for a long time, but I hardly knew anything about the Little Guy except for the fact that he had graduated from the Terlemezyan Art College. He had been trying to sell his work in the park for two weeks but had barely managed to sell a couple of paintings. I had almost paid off my debt, only a thousand or two thousand drams remained. One day, when I was returning home from class, I spotted a painting that did not seem to be any different from the others at first glance. It had the same clouds on it, but this painting seemed to be brighter; the colors on it shimmered.

"Is that a new painting?" I asked and, seeing the Little Guy nod in affirmation, I added a joke, "So these must be a sorrowful person's clouds?"

"No, they're a happy person's clouds," he replied enthusiastically, "I painted it three days ago."

It was the first time that one of his paintings was not named after a sad or depressive state.

"It's because I was happy when I painted it," he added.

That was the last conversation I had with the Little Guy, I did not see him in the park the following day. I thought he would come along, since I had not yet fully paid him back, but he did not show up.

It was the nineteenth of December when the first snowflakes started to float down upon the city. Our exams were over and I had nothing to do, so I roamed aimlessly about the city. I was walking down Teryan Street to the Opera, from where I planned to walk to the Cascade and then get home quickly because the snowflakes were growing larger and it was quite cold. I had just walked past the Opera building when I saw an old man with a painting in his hand who wanted to cross the street. The painting was not covered with a cloth and the man seemed to be in no hurry to protect it from the snow. I thought that it was probably a piece of junk, or perhaps a fresh, unpainted canvas, but it was a strange sight nonetheless. I crossed the streets and had only taken a few steps when I saw a woman walking with a child and, once again, holding a painting in her hand. By the time I got to the Cascade, the snow had started to settle on the pavement. A group of people standing in the distance caught my attention; they had formed a circle and kept growing in size. I turned and started to walk in their direction. I had not yet reached them when the crowd seemed to pull back instantaneously and the Little Guy appeared in the middle. It all happened so quickly that I could not grasp any of it. He was moving his arms in the air, waving them in an unusual way, as if trying to prevent the snowflakes from touching the ground, as if trying to send them back up to the sky. He was picking up snow from the ground and throwing it upward, all the while shouting,

"Don't come here, you'll get dirty. Don't come here, I said!"

He was crying and shouting. Then, he took something out of his pocket and hurled it in the direction of the people who had gathered; the coins he had thrown fell into the snow.

"Take all this," he shouted and then took off his shirt, also throwing it to the crowd. The people withdrew, many of them kept a wary distance and some left the scene entirely. For a moment, I felt like walking up to him and calming him down, but I hesitated. The Little Guy was crying and swearing; he had taken off all his clothes and stood there naked, but he stubbornly kept trying to stop the snow from falling. I joined the people who stood some distance away from him. The police soon arrived and put him in their car, taking him away. After that incident, I learned that the Little Guy lived in extreme poverty, sleeping under the Lambada Bridge and, on the day I saw him for the last time, he had apparently given away all his paintings to random people and gone insane. Some people said that he hadn't given them away, he had sold them for five hundred drams each, or something like that. But all conversation on this topic soon ceased, everyone forgot the Little Guy.

The painting I bought, which I never managed to pay for in full, now hangs on the wall in our living room, occupying the most visible of spots in our home. This painting by the Little Guy awes all our guests, who stare at it for a long time. But none of them notices that, behind the bright, shining clouds, the snowflakes keep falling.

ONE PERSON'S CITY

Dedicated to my friend Tigran Kirakosyan

Every evening, when the mute and unmoving heat softened a little, and people flooded the street like ants, he would hold a box of pens and walk from one street to the next in the area around the Opera building, saying, "These are good pens, really good ones… Take three for a hundred drams…" with the hope of grabbing the attention of passers-by. He would walk from one person to another all evening, holding out the box… But it was rare for a person not to avoid the old man and reject his pleas; just a few people took pity on him. Although he was fifty-three years old, his ample beard and worn-out clothes made him look like an old man. He always wore the same clothes – a gray, slightly loose pair of pants and a thick, drab coat that went all the way down to his knees, its color faded in certain spots, resembling milky islets to anyone who looked at it…

The old man had an unusual habit. Every time there was a new performance at the Opera and its poster appeared on the fence of the building, he would walk up to the ticket booth with that unhurried pace of his and inquire how much the tickets cost. There had never been an occasion when he had bought a ticket, but he would always make sure to check the price. Why did he do this?

The story I'm about to tell you took place when I was working at the book stall nearby. On Mashtots Avenue, right next to the Opera, there's a medium-sized booth selling books – that was where I worked. It's difficult to imagine a more suitable or pleasant job for someone like me – a small, comfortable space surrounded by books. I would read all day and had discovered a range of foreign authors I had not heard about earlier and, judging by what those books cost, I could not expect to possess any of them in the near future. The only inconvenience that kept me from plunging completely into this realm of ecstasy were the customers that showed up once in a while and, of course, Sofa. The people who came had all kinds of personalities and temperaments you could imagine. It was obvious that many of them simply had the need to speak out and they would just ask a few questions, talk about the impression that one book or the other left on them, after which they would say thank you and disappear. But all of my customers combined could still not match up to Sofa. Sofa had been selling tickets at the Opera booth for a long time – she was a petite woman past forty, always neatly dressed, wearing high heels and make-up, with all kinds of accessories and antique-like silver items on her hands. But the most important thing that seemed to complete her image as an active person who was constantly on the move was the fact that she was extremely talkative. Sofa would talk incessantly, without so much as a hint of a pause, about everything under the sun. And because a twist of fate had meant that the two of us worked in the same territory (I would sit in one corner of the booth and she would take the other to sell tickets, with nothing separating our two sections), I was condemned to hearing her talk the whole day. She would talk about the places she had been fortunate enough to visit at a young age, about how she had miraculously avoided falling into a valley during one of her hikes, she recalled how she had lost a lemon-yellow coat, which she had forgotten at a Dolphin Show the day she had bought it after going with a friend to see dolphins for the first time in her life, she would never forget her daughters' weddings… She talked about all kinds of things, but what distracted me the most from my books was her way of commenting on everyone who walked past the booth, sharing what knowledge she had of them.

"Look, look, it's Rubo," she would say each time with undying enthusiasm, "Our ballet star – tall, handsome, that's what a dancer should look like! You should have seen him dance in the role of Spartak! But they don't appreciate him. He'll pack up and leave for England soon, like the rest of them. They really value our dancers there, they know what a good dancer is worth… He's just a bit careless, they've only just taken the cast off his arm, he had broken a finger during rehearsal. He always ends up hurting himself, but nevertheless…"

"And there's Misha! He's one of the guards – a really interesting guy, you know? He's got two university degrees, if you sit down and talk with him a bit, he can provide enough material for you to write a book, I'm serious! He's always broke, though, always asking me for cash from the machine until he gets his salary at the end of the month… He's been married and divorced three times…"

Anyone she knew or had heard something about provided endless material for Sofa to discuss as soon as they happened to walk past our window. She knew everyone, from the conductors, singers, and dancers, to the accountants and guards at the Opera. Every time, I was filled with a childish surprise at how she could know so many people, and how she was aware of all these details of their lives. She spoke with particular care and tenderness about her regular customers, who would consider it their sacred duty to come to the Opera, even if they had arrived from different parts of the world. I noticed how she always gave them special treatment and referred to them by name; even before the customer had walked up to the booth, she would open the window immediately and say their name, greeting them warmly. On the rare occasion when she could not recall it or mistakenly used another name, she treated it like a real tragedy, as if she had made the gravest of professional errors…

And so, the stories kept coming, one after the other, and they seemed to be endless. Sofa would talk all day and, if I wasn't available for any reason, she would engage with the other customers. If they did not encourage her either, there was always the phone (she would often have long, winding conversations on the phone) and, no matter how strongly I wanted to read a book, I was embarrassed to tell her that I needed quiet. However, to my surprise, my torture did not last long and events unfolded such that the silence I had been dreaming about was suddenly thrust upon me; renovation work started at the Opera and the ticket counter was temporarily closed, liberating me of Sofa and her incessant stories. It's difficult for me to recall any other time when I had read with such enthusiasm – I would finish one book and immediately start the next, often taking them home; the period of renovation at the Opera would have undoubtedly become one of my fondest memories if not for an unexpected encounter…

It was a regular day, just like any other. The sun had covered the city with its pale rays, spreading tedium on the streets, while on the territory of the Opera, the noise from Mashtots Avenue could be heard as always, and people kept going past the booth in an unending flow without noticing me or the books. Suddenly, someone tapped on the window. And there he stood in front of the booth – gray, a man with eyes that were always tense, and ragged clothes, his age long lost in his abundant beard. Assuming that he was just another beggar and was about to ask for money, I opened the window and was about to hand him the coins I had in my breast pocket when the old man pointed at the display window and asked for Levon Khechoyan's *King Arshak and Drastamat the Eunuch*. His head bowed before the book, he leafed through it at an unhurried pace, and the moldy smell coming from him was so suffocating that I could not stand near the window. But I could not allow myself to get too far, I was afraid he would slip away with the book. He continued to flip through its pages, not noticing me. While the old man was submerged in the labyrinth of history, I looked at the opening of the collar of his shirt, below which I could see that he was wearing shirts of various colors and style, all on top of each other. Once again, I was struck by wonder at why homeless people always wore so much clothing, even on hot summer days…

"I've read his *Olibanum Trees*," he said, raising his eyes, "But I haven't heard of this one, this is the first time I've seen this book."

He said nothing else, then returned the book, thanked me, and left, but this was more than enough to get me thinking about him. After I left, I found myself unable to continue reading the book I had dropped, I could not figure out how he could have known about Khechoyan and his book… I had seen this old man before, I would always watch from the booth window how he would hold a box of pens in his hand every evening and approach passers-by. When he grew tired, he would sit on one of the benches under the trees and watch the infinite stream of people flowing by. But he had caught my attention when I noticed how he would always come up to the ticket counter every time a new performance was due to premier at the Opera, asking the price every time but never buying a ticket. I thought he had mental health issues and I would probably have remained convinced of that if not for that encounter. The old man was definitely not crazy, the insane are always betrayed by the look in their eyes, but his eyes were far from mad…

The old man continued to be at the focus of my attention for a while, but I would probably have forgotten him and that encounter soon, if he had not ended up reminding me of himself. A week had gone by when he walked up to the booth once again. He stood there in front of the booth and kept looking for a long time, his gray eyes lazily sliding from one book to the other, and I got the impression that he was looking for something, but did not dare tap the window.

"I'm sorry, could you pass me Khechoyan's book?" he finally said after tapping on the window and, pointing at a bench nearby, he added, "I'll read it on that bench over there and then return it at the end of the day..."

It's hard to say how I would have acted if I had had time to think it over, but everything happened so quickly at that moment. No matter how clearly I understood that I did not have the right to do that, that I was not allow to give him the book to read, I was unable to refuse him. The old man thanked me several times and stepped away, settling down into a corner of the bench and starting to read. With every page he turned over, I felt a greater sense of regret at what I had done, I thought that the book would smell like a sewer after he was done... I had already come to terms with the fact that I would no longer be able to sell that book and that it would be coming out of my paycheck. I had decided that I would not take it back from him when he tried to return it, I would tell him to keep it as a gift. That way, I would have done something nice while also ridding myself of the old man. But subsequent events took a different turn. As agreed, he walked up to the booth at the end of the day and held out the book, once again thanking me several times, and I had not yet managed to say anything when he began to tell me his thoughts on what he had read. Strangely enough, when I try to find an adequate way to describe the old man's words now, all I can think of as a suitable comparison is a tree. His words were truly like a tree, which gave off branches as it rose up, seemingly infinite in its height. Soon, he had transitioned from Khechoyan to Hrant Matevosyan, then to Ryūnosuke Akutagawa, Kafka... One author followed the other, and all I could do was listen, absorbing everything he said.

That was how my conversations with the old man started. Every day, after he had finished his work, he would walk up and ask for a book, then settle down in the bench. At the end of the day, he would return the book and we would start to talk.

"Have you noticed how many crows there are in the city? It wasn't like this before. The crows nowadays are different, too, they're completely black... Take a closer look. They have nests on all the trees, especially on

Sayat-Nova Street. If the city were to go quiet for a moment, the noise they make would be enough to drive anyone mad…"

"I'm constantly upset, my mind is always tense; when everything is going badly, I'm scared and try to find a way to fix the situation. When things are good, I'm scared then too, I feel like something bad will happen at any moment…"

"Crazy people take longer to grow old…"

"Look at the face of any of these passers-by – you can easily tell our people apart from those who have moved here. Ours are always in a hurry, they don't have any time. The people from here don't really live, the people from here spend all of their lives preparing to die…"

"There's something majestic but also sad in migratory birds, it always makes me sad to watch them…"

His words grew bolder from one conversation to the next. It was as if so much had built up inside him and he had finally found someone to whom he could talk about it all. He talked about different things, expressing his opinion or position. After he left, I would make a few notes in my pad of the things he had said, in the hope that I would use them one day when writing a story…

Time flew by unnoticed like the pages of a book and the month of May arrived, bringing day after day of rainfall. I would either sit in the booth and read a book, or look out the window for hours. It was interesting to watch the color fade from the day and to see the treetops sway. The wind would stir up the dried leaves, resulting in small whirlwinds of dusty mass on the sidewalks. And when the rain started, Mashtots Avenue—which was always full of people—would empty out at once, revealing a dwarfish, black figure in the distance. It was only in the rain that Rodin's sculpture could be seen from the booth window. Every time the street was deserted, its gray shape would appear and an inexplicable feeling would come over me, as if the dwarf was looking out at the street and enjoying the emptiness surrounding him… Only the old man violated this emptiness, curled up on a bench next to a tree with his box of pens by his side, his scowl making it difficult to guess what he was thinking. Every time I tried to sum up what I knew about the old man, I realized that I did not really know anything. And although it had been quite a long time that we had been speaking to each other, I had not dared ask about his past. The past was a closed subject for him, but the more I thought about it, the more I felt a desire to delve into the old man's past. The only thing that surprised me was how Sofa had never mentioned anything about him…

The sky was surprisingly clear that day, the sun had finally come out after a period of rain, people were walking about the city streets, and the old man stood as always on Mashtots Avenue with his box of pens. I would glance out the window from time to time to dispel boredom and, when I had turned to look out on one of those occasions, a suspicious scene quickly grabbed my eye. The old man stood motionless in the middle of the street. He no longer moved from one pedestrian to the other with his box held out. People kept walking past him and everything was in motion except for him, coiled up in his worn-out overcoat in that storm of people, sounds, and colors. It was like time had come to a standstill for him… Thinking that he was perhaps not feeling well, I was getting ready to walk up to him, when the old man suddenly turned around and began to walk away rapidly, as if he had taken offense at something, and it was only then I noticed that the box he was holding was empty. That was the last day I saw the old man, he no longer appeared after that. All kinds of things went through my mind, but I did not want to think that I would not see him again. Perhaps I would continue believing that we would meet again if not for my conversation with Sofa. A short while after the old man's disappearance, Sofa returned. Renovation work at the Opera building had ended and the ticket counter had reopened. I was unexpectedly happy, Sofa's return was a surprise, I had even come to miss her endless stories and chats. On the very day of her return, I asked her about the old man who always asked about the ticket price but never bought one. Sofa, as always, knew everything. When she heard my question, she grew sadder, saying that I had asked something she did not want to discuss, but she would answer anyway. She said that the old man had been an opera singer once, and had taught at the Conservatory. But then, for some reason, he had lost everything and ended up on the streets… Sofa recalled a few scenes she had witnessed involving the old man, or stories she had heard from acquaintances. But the last thing she said seared itself into my memory and I wish I had never heard it.

"They say that one of his former students at the Conservatory spotted him outside and gave a woman some money to buy all his pens, so that his teacher would not have to spend more time on the street… He noticed his student and realized what had happened, and no longer showed up on the street the next day, the day after that, nor the third day… He was found later at a bus stop, dead…"

Sofa talked about the old man without considering for a moment that I had known him, or that I had seen him on that day she had described… I listened without interrupting her, trying to remember all the things she had said. When I looked out into the street, it was deserted–absorbed in conversation, we had not noticed that it had started to rain. As it poured down, the dwarf appeared in the distance again, joyfully watching the street once more. The only difference was that nobody violated the emptiness any more…

TWO SILHOUETTES

The front page of the newspaper carried a warning announcement from the police that had shocked the city residents.

"To collectors and admirers of old paintings. If you come across a painting of two silhouettes, with writing on the other side that says 'Don't take anything from bad people,' please report this to the nearest police station. Do not keep the painting with you for any reason, it could pose a danger to your life…"

New details soon surfaced. The strange painting, it emerged, had a dramatic story. All twenty people who had obtained it had each jumped out a window and died a short while after it came into their possession. Police detectives were unable to find an explanation, but the antique experts supporting the investigation were convinced that the painting was unusual, it could drive people insane…

When the painting was found, the police department imprisoned an object for the first time in history. Experts presented the sole explanation they could come up with to the court – the painting must have born witness to a savage murder, perhaps the person killed had been its first owner, or the painter whose brush had created this accursed piece that had taken place right before had absorbed the negative energy and accumulated the fear of death within it. Ever since then, it would pass on the human torture it had concealed inside itself to the next owner who took possession…

After the investigation, a report in the newspaper that listed the twenty victims also mentioned for the first time the name of a man who had managed to survive, thanks to whom the police had found the painting. That man was Gurgen.

It all began with a phone call. Sitting on a couch, he was leafing through his copy of *Antique* magazine as usual—the latest one he had received in the mail following his twenty faithful years as a subscriber—when his phone rang.

"Yes?" he said dispassionately after he had placed the receiver at his ear.

"Hello, hello?" the male voice at the other end of the line said, constantly feeling the need to repeat his "hello"-s because of the poor connection. "Hello, can you hear me? I'd like to talk to Tigran."

"You've got the wrong number, there is no Tigran here."

Gurgen hung up and settled back into his couch with a dissatisfied mumble, but the phone rang again before he could pick up his magazine.

"Hello, hello? I'd like to talk to Gurgen," said the same voice.

"This is Gurgen. Who am I talking to?" he asked in confusion, surprised by how the same caller was now asking for him.

"My name is Ruben… I hear you are a big fan of antique items…"

The man spoke distractedly, there was a clear urgency to his words. He said that he had some medals, coins and other old items that he was in a hurry to sell.

"I have to sell it all today and get it over with, I have a flight to catch tomorrow… To be honest, I'm not very good at understanding how far they date back or what they are. Let me tell you my address. It would be great if you could drop by today…"

After he had hung up, Gurgen looked with some doubt at the paper on which he had noted the address. This was not the first time a stranger had called and asked him to buy some old items. There were barely any antique sellers in the city apart from him and he had not bought anything or asked around. Everyone knew him and his preferences, so the call he had received that morning had not come as a surprise. And there had been many occasions on which he had returned home after a call like this one with some "valuable loot."

They said that everything began after the death of his wife, when she had passed away unexpectedly one morning, never waking up. He had started collecting old items from that day onward, and nobody could say what exactly the connection was between these occurrences. His reticent and maverick nature further fanned the flames of people's imagination. There were stories suggesting that he had confessed on one occasion to how a feeling of loss and emptiness would overcome him every time he returned home after his wife's death. Unable to make peace with the situation, he had decided to fill that void by collecting old items… People said all kinds of things, especially after the story with the famous painting, but one thing was for sure – his house was full of all kinds of little items that had come from various periods and nations around the world. Although they were not particularly valuable, they would make him as happy and proud as a little child. Every time after lunch, when he was in a good mood, he would clean his table carefully, wipe the surface with a moist cloth, and place the items on it next to each other, studying them meticulously for hours, comparing them to each other. He took particular pleasure in his collection of medals from Fascist Germany, because those had been the most difficult to procure, and not everyone in town could claim a collection of this kind.

He was playing around with the paper bearing the address between his fingers as he stood in the middle of the living room and pondered whether or not to visit the stranger, when Adada slid across the railing of the balcony and ended up on the floor.

"Are you here? I was getting ready to start without you. Come on then, let's see what we've got for you," he smiled as he noticed the cat and, dropping the paper on the table, he went into the kitchen. Adada tried not to fall far behind his master.

This friendship between Gurgen and the cat had gone on for many years, and the furry animal kept him company at the dinner table every day. In the past, he had never liked cats, to put it mildly, and had rushed to shoo off any of these creatures as soon as one appeared on the balcony. His wife had not been a big fan either because they ruined her laundry by touching it with their grubby paws or scratching it. All the cats in the building courtyard knew what awaited them on the third-floor balcony hidden beneath the grapevine, and they did their best to stay away. Adada would have received the same treatment no doubt, if not for an unusual incident. It had been a regular summer day (his fifth summer without his wife), when Gurgen had come home and heard mewing shortly afterwards, which kept repeating from time to time. Thinking that a cat had snuck in while he had been away, he walked from room to room, investigating every nook and cranny. No matter how hard he tried to understand where the mewing was coming from, he failed. It was as if the animal was mocking him, knowing that Gurgen was pursuing it, it was fleeing from one end of the house to the other. Eventually, he realized to his great surprise that the sound was coming from inside the kitchen wall. It turned out that one of his neighbors had been doing some work on the roof that day and had forgotten to shut the ventilation shaft. A newborn kitten had fallen into the hole and come to a stop right at the level of the third floor. At first, he decided to do nothing (what could he do – tear down a wall to save a kitten?) He simply needed to wait a couple of days until the creature exhausted itself and died. But the kitten did not give up two days later, nor on the third. It was running out of strength and its mews for help grew weaker, turning into the creak of a door, then the sound that comes from faucets when the water supply is cut off. After that, they turned into a strange nasal intonation that sounded like "adada" which really did not even have a distant resemblance to mewing. He could no longer bear it; there wasn't a corner in the house where the sound could not be heard. He decided to rescue the cat; there was nothing else he could do. The only way to do it that he could think of at the moment was to make a rope of gauze cloth and lower it into the kitchen ventilation shaft. He thought that the creature could easily hold on to it with its claws, and he would then be able to raise it up. But it turned out not to be so easy. After many unsuccessful attempts and several hours of torture, it became clear that it would not work – the kitten had no strength left and it would hold on to the rope, but as soon Gurgen started to raise it, it could no longer hold on and kept falling off. Perhaps in another case, these attempts would have been enough for Gurgen to conclude that he had tried his best and given up on trying to rescue the creature. But the accursed "adada" stubbornly continued to be heard, it seemed to ring in his ears. Even when he was not home, he could hear it over his shoulder, and it made him feel guilty, he felt sorry for the kitten… After several more days of unsuccessful attempts, the rescue was finally accomplished. In that time, Gurgen regularly attached pieces of sausage to the rope and lowered it to the kitten, thinking that this would help the creature regain its strength and hold on better. But, deep down, he did not really believe that he would succeed, and when the kitten's black head, covered in dust, eventually peeked out of the ventilation shaft, Gurgen's joy was sincere and even childlike. He could not hide a smile as he looked at the jet-black cat with green eyes, curled up in a corner and watching him with eyes full of panic; it seemed difficult to believe that the same creature had seemed condemned and was barely managing to fight for its life a short while ago. It had recoiled in a way that served as a warning – it was ready to defend itself against anyone who dared approach it; the only sound it made, instead of mewing, was that constant "adada". That soon changed. After it greedily quenched its thirst, it began to sneeze and then cough—its throat seemed to be covered in dust and soot—after which it began to mew again. Gurgen decided that he had to take the cat out of the apartment immediately, before it could dirty up the place. But he felt sorry for it at the last moment and decided that it was not worth putting it out at night. He would let it stay for one day and then release it. That one day turned into two, three, then into a week, and soon he had not realized how he grew accustomed to the creature's presence, acting as if he bore responsibility for it. And he named the cat Adada, to highlight the strange sound that had led to the cat's rescue.

While Adada munched on the remainder of her food, Gurgen leaned back into his couch after finishing his meal and continued to think. He could not forget the call. It was obvious that the caller knew nothing about old items and it was possible that he had some valuable objects. On the other hand, one could not rule out that it would end up being just a bunch of scrap metal, as was often the case. Nevertheless, after hesitating for a long time, he decided to go and see for himself. He put on his coat and a broad-rimmed hat, picked up the paper with the address from the table and walked towards the door. He was at the place an hour later. From the first minute of their conversation, Ruben seemed to be a pleasant guy. That short and plump man spoke rapidly in person, just as he had on the phone. He kept repeating the fact that he had a flight the following day, and his words rushed out so rapidly that Gurgen was barely able to keep up. When Gurgen walked into the garage, his throat was immediately assaulted by the smell of humidity – fungi covered the walls in patterns that looked like carpets. As he threw a quick glance to scan the space, Ruben kicked aside the box fragments that lay at his feet and walked up to a set of items placed separately in plastic bags in a corner, then returned with one of them in his hand. The bag had medals and coins that, as Gurgen has suspected, proved to be of no interest. For a moment, he even regretted that he had come, but then managed to find a few valuable pieces; he was preparing to leave after paying for them, when the man took out a painting from among the items in the corner. No matter how much he insisted that he had no interest in paintings, Ruben asked him to take it. He said that he was giving it to him as a present, once again explaining that his flight was due to leave the following day and that he had to vacate the garage, by taking the painting Gurgen would be doing him a huge favor. In this way, he was forced to accept the gift.

It was evening by the time Gurgen reached home. He changed his clothes and, after a refreshing splash of cold water, he took his bag of freshly procured objects to the living room with childlike excitement so that he could examine his new possessions in detail. After the medals and coins, he took the painting out of the bag. It depicted two silhouettes walking together on a street surrounded by leafless autumn trees, and a blinding light could be seen in the distance. The painting was dominated by cool colors – dark blue and gray, but it was a pleasant piece overall. He turned the piece around this way and that in the hope of finding the artist's signature but could only find some puzzling writing that said "Don't take anything from bad people." He considered it unimportant and decided to hang his new possession in the living room. The painting was an unusual one and seemed to grab one's attention immediately after entering the room. But it soon seemed quite normal, as if it had fused into the room and the items around it. Moreover, over time he noticed that the painting had endeared itself to him, there was something attractive about it, he would stare at it for a long time and feel happy that he had taken it.

Life went on as usual. Everything was the same except for the surprisingly colorful dreams that Gurgen started having. He had never had such dreams before; in fact, he had not dreamed much before that at all. It was just a few scenes at first that would otherwise have been deemed lost forever in the depths of his childhood. He would see their old house, the apricot tree, the hospital wall… And every time he woke up, his heart would melt at the thought that he had left the sunshine of his life in the paths he walked as a child. And so, night became his favorite time of the day, when images from previous years would appear before him one after the other. They were so real, so tangible, that he often awoke with tears in his eyes. He had dreams every night for around a month, but soon one of them began to recur. The frequently repeating dream seemed to gradually push the others aside, and soon remained the only one. Gurgen could not explain it – every time he closed his eyes, he would see the same thing. It would repeat with perfect precision—not a single detail would change—and was different from the other dreams, which had been memories. He would appear in a place that looked like a garden, somewhere he had never been before, and when he started to walk along a path there, his dream would end and he would wake up with a start, drenched in sweat. Every time, he would wake up exhausted, and feeling as if he had a fever. He was sure that this was the result of his bad eating habits and the fact that he would get stressed at every little thing, and that it would pass in a little while. He was in no hurry to see a doctor. The dream seemed to last longer with each passing night, and it became harder and harder to wake up. The next time Gurgen's eyelids grew heavy, the dream absorbed him completely.

He was walking and the shadows of the trees were sliding off his shoulders, he felt like the path would bend at any moment and the end would come within sight, but the garden seemed boundless. Suddenly, he heard a noise, like the sound of a *dhol* and he started walking in that direction until he confirmed it. There was a group of several dozen people standing in a circle, watching a young tightrope walker performing on a rope stretched at a height between two poles, while a man with a sunburned face played the *dhol,* slightly apart from the rest. The young man wore red from head to toe as he skipped about on the rope and performed other tricks. Gurgen walked up and started watching the young man's agile moves like everyone else, when he suddenly saw his wife among the crowd. She was standing in the front row and watching the young man, she had not noticed him. There was a remarkable expression of peace on her face, her eyes directly serenely upwards. While he tried to break through the crowd and get closer to her, his wife and another person broke off from the rest and started to walk down the path. No matter how hard he tried to catch up with them, he could not, his feet would not obey him. He tried to catch a glimpse of his wife's companion. Watching the man from behind, his gait seemed very familiar to him, he had definitely seen him somewhere, but he found himself unable to recall any of it. The distance between them grew larger and the shadows from the trees grew longer, stretching like talons to block his path. He noticed that his wife and the man quickened their pace, they were hurrying towards the blinding light in the distance. He starting rushing too. The light was so close now that he could not see anything, the man and the woman had become two silhouettes. He tried not to let them out of his sight, stubbornly striving to catch up. When they were just a few paces apart, a small shadow fell across his path. At first, he did not understand what it was, and it took him a few seconds to realize that it was a cat. Jet-black from head to toe, the cat unhurriedly walked across the path, then stopped in a corner and began to mew. He had stopped and did not know what to do. He was trying to continue down the path, but found himself unable to do so, as if the little creature was holding him back. He shot a glance in the direction of the light and saw that the silhouettes had stopped as well, they were waiting for him. But he could not manage to walk around the cat, he seemed rooted to his spot. The mewing had become unbearable, the cat stared into his eyes and mewed endlessly, and the sound seemed to come closer and closer to him, as if ringing in his head. Soon, everything around him seemed to slip away and the image melted like wax. He tried to stop it from happening, struggling to hold it in his arms, but when he raised his eyes to see if his wife and the stranger were still waiting, he noticed with horror that the man standing next to his wife had his own face, it was him… He woke up at once.

When the dream had snatched itself off his eyes, Gurgen was standing at the railing of the balcony, just one step away from falling off. He greedily swallowed the cold air and could not comprehend what had happened. Before him lay the city, slowly waking up and getting ready to start the day. Next to him, in a corner of the railing, Adada stared at him and kept mewing.

A SMALL, GRAY SUITCASE

Those who often walk along the streets of Yerevan have come across him for sure – he was a man of medium height, neither fat nor thin, with a forehead that had gone brown under the sun, and gray, concerned eyes. You could recognize him from afar based on the way he dressed; he always wore the same clothes – the old pants his deceased father used to wear and the dark jacket that had kept well, in contrast to the pants. Nobody ever found out his name or who he was. All that was known about him was how he walked alone on the streets of Yerevan all day holding his small, gray suitcase, never raising his eyes above ground level, as if searching for something – something very important and dear.

He closed the apartment door and putting a hand on the bannister of the stairwell, walked downstairs at an unhurried pace. It was a bright day and a kind of inexplicable and irrational kindness seemed to be floating in the air. He got on a bus and quickly took a seat at one of the windows, then took a piece of paper and pencil from his suitcase and looked outside. His eyebrows furrowed, his eyes were tense, as if he were doing something very important by staring out the window that way, concerned that he might miss something, that something might slip by his watchful gaze. He began to take notes on the paper, the pencil slid messily and left behind jumbled, illegible letters. He did not look away from the window, except to turn and stare angrily at the back of the driver from time to time before mumbling to himself and resuming his observations out the window. The people in the bus would sometimes glance at his window to see what had caught his attention in this way, but they found nothing unusual and recoiled back into their thoughts, continuing their journey with the numbing sound of the engine in their heads.

He got off the bus and walked along Abovyan Street, never raising his head above ground level, as usual. It was one of his favorite streets because it was always full of people and he had discovered some of the best walks on that street. He had already spent many years on that strange and unknown hobby – he studied the way people walked and collected them. It was a whole world that belonged only to him. He had created it and nobody could gain entry there except for him. Every afternoon, he would roam around the city with the suitcase in his hand, walking from street to street and affixing his gaze on people's gait. He recognized people from the way they walked and he often smiled to himself when he saw a gait he recognized. For him, people did not exist, only the way they walked did, and these gaits were all interesting and different from each other.

He walked leisurely past Moscow Cinema and directed his feet towards Republic Square. One would think that there were so many people around him and as many different gaits, but it was all so boring. He was looking for a new, so far unseen way of walking. He did not have a clear picture of what he was seeking, but he was convinced that he would recognize it when he saw it. Tired, he sat down on a bench on a corner, angry at the pedestrians in a sincere and childlike manner for stubbornly concealing their best manner of walking from him. He opened his suitcase and carefully took out his important papers, then began to peruse them. Those numbered sheets were his children, the meaning of his life. They bore the best gaits he had ever seen. His eyes sped over the drawings and words that only he could understand, and his heart began to get ticklish under his chest. The gaits he read about appeared before his eyes and he recalled every detail and every movement, gaining a sense of inexplicable satisfaction. The manners of walking were described word for word, not a single movement had evaded his eye. Here was one he had discovered near Charents Street, and this other one had been spotted on Tumanyan Street… The gaits were different and did not repeat and he had his own explanation for each one. Each one of them concealed a secret or something specific about the temperament of the given person and he, only he, knew all those secrets.

The streets had already lit up their yellow lights, he had walked along the whole city but had not managed to find what he was seeking. He was now walking unhurriedly toward the bus stop while continuing to observe how pedestrians around him walked. But the light from the street lamps was already weak and his eyesight had started to let him down. The shadows created illusions and he was unable to observe the gaits of the people around him. At one point, the way one person was walking caught his attention and, straining his eyes, he managed to isolate it and grab the opportunity. But after staring for a while he muttered, "I've blanked out" and turned his head, continuing to walk in disappointment. He had noticed a long time ago that people who had come from villages—or, as he called them, the "mountain folk"—would cast their legs further forward when walking, much further than average. City-dwellers, on the other hand, or those who had moved to the city a long time ago, walked with smaller and more careful steps...

He sat on the bench at the bus stop waiting for public transport. Several buses had already gone past without stopping, but that was not unusual. It often happened that when the driver saw how he was dressed, he would pretend not to notice him... Suddenly, he noticed an unusual movement out of the corner of his eye and he turned towards the underground pedestrian crossing. His heart began to beat rapidly. Could it be... He strained his eyes, trying to make sure that he had not made yet another mistake... No, this was what he was looking for, this was the walk he had been seeking for such a long time! He got up quickly and threw himself into the underground pedestrian crossing after the walk. He was afraid he would not be able to catch up, that he would let it slip from his field of vision, but he made it. The crossing was deserted, dark, and the walk floated in front of him in a small body that leaned slightly forward, but kept its hips emphatically loose. There was a lack of responsibility, a levity in those movements, and he felt an inexplicable familiarity about the whole thing, as if all of this had already happened; it was as if the walk was trying to nudge his memory, to remind him of something old and very warm. He was almost running, striving to understand the inexplicable familiarity, to watch the walk from as closely as possible and memorize each movement, but he kept moving further away. An invisible force was pulling him back, increasing the space between him and the walk. He suddenly noticed that something was changing, the walk was gathering pace, the reddish shoes were tapping the ground in panic, clicking as if their last remaining hope was on the line, like the shoes were growing lighter and lighter and that the feet would stop touching the ground and start to soar, going up a flight of transparent, invisible stairs.

"Don't leave me alone," he shouted despite himself, realizing that the walk was departing.

In one second, the walk slid up the stairs and walked out of the underground pedestrian crossing. He gathered his strength and rushed, sensing that when he emerged from the crossing he would be near, he would be right there…

"Leave me alone or I'll scream…" the words were spoken in a trembling voice and they froze him on the spot, nailing him to the ground. Everything dissipated in a moment and the delirium slipped away from his eyes. All that remained was a girl in reddish shoes standing before him, her eyes shimmering in fear, gazing at him like a cornered animal.

"I… I…" he tried to say something, to explain himself, but he could not. He turned and began to run down the stairs. He could still see the walk before his eyes, but he could not understand what had happened and what the panic-filled words of the girl meant. That was not so important at the moment. All that he was thinking about was his new discovery – the new walk. He imagined himself putting a number on a new sheet of paper that described the new walk and placing it carefully in his suitcase next to the other walks (he always numbered the papers because he constantly thought that he was missing some of them. He would take them out of the suitcase and carefully place them next to each other, counting. It was as if that constant counting brought serenity and numbness to his nerves, and a short while later he considered himself an important person).

He turned around and made sure that nobody was following him. He stopped and began to hungrily breathe in the air of the underground crossing. He was afraid; of what, he did not know, but he *was* afraid. And when he decided that he did not trust his memory and needed to note down the walk as quickly as possible, it was as if someone shouted inside his head – "the suitcase!" And it was only then he realized that the suitcase was not in his hand. A shiver went through his whole body and his heart began to flutter like a fish thrown out of the sea. He stood there, by one of the walls of the deserted underground pedestrian crossing and could not move. He could not believe that the suitcase that had always been inseparable from him was not in his hand.

"I must have left it on the bench," he said to himself and began to run like he had lost his mind. He recalled that before he had noticed the walk, when he was sitting on the bench at the bus stop, the suitcase had been by his side. He was certain that it would still be there, placed on the bench… But when he emerged from the underground crossing, the bus stop was empty, the suitcase was gone. He could not believe his eyes. He walked up to the bench and ran his fingers over the spot where the suitcase had been just a short while ago. When it sunk in that the suitcase was really gone, he threw himself with tears in his eyes at the people walking past and began asking them to give back his suitcase. The people thought that he was crazy and moved away, but he kept walking up to them and saying, "I'm a miserable man – a poor, miserable man," as he begged them to return his suitcase.

The sun had started to rise when he got home. His whole body was in pain, his legs had been drained of strength, he had sweated so much that his clothes were sticking to his body. He opened the door and walked in. The house and its silence immediately absorbed his bent body. He had run across town the whole night, he had searched everywhere, all the bus stop benches, but he had not found his small, gray suitcase. As soon as he got home, he rushed from room to room. He was searching. He knew that it would not be at home, he remembered leaving it on the bus stop bench, but he could not resist searching here. He walked silently into the living room and, collapsing into the couch, began crying like a child. He wanted to break something, to hit the couch with his fists, but his body would not respond, he had no strength left. He remained lying there for a few days, getting up only to drink water and use the bathroom, but he did not get up on the last day. He would not eat anything; he felt no hunger. On one occasion when he was walking to the kitchen to drink water, he glanced at the small, oval mirror that hung above the refrigerator, and he was startled. Two gray eyes, flickering like candle flame, stared back at him from the mirror… He realized at once that this was not his own gaze, it was his father's. It was his father who would look at him that way when he lay in his bed, dying silently…

And he lay there on the couch now, neither asleep nor awake. His eyes seemed to be open, but the images and the movement he saw were like a dream – a warm, very warm dream. The suitcase kept appearing before his eyes and, in his mind, he ran his fingers over the gray surface covered in scratches. It was cold, it felt very cold to him, and his fingers would then touch the worn-out, faded corners, and then the silver buckles… He saw images of walks before his eyes, and he recalled each movement, every detail, and he noted it all down greedily, recording the walk on a sheet of paper, laughing, joyous.

"A walk with shuffling heels, heavy and proud, the feet always tense, obviously weak and unenthusiastic, emphatically broad and… They're not lost, they're not lost," he would run through them in his mind like a tongue-twister and seem to slowly regain control of himself and return to reality. But it would not last long, his mind would throw off its shackles again and take him down a different path. The walk rushing into the pedestrian crossing appeared before his eyes, and he was running after it again, his heart was beating faster… He held out his hand, seeking to touch the walk, but the image would change at the last instant, and his father would appear before his eyes. His memory kept playing back different scenes, it was happening very quickly, he had no perception of time. He had lost his understanding of time, all he knew was that his father was close, so very close… Ah, he has walked in the house. He runs up and starts rummaging through his father's coat pockets. He knows that this is where he hides the candy, that's what he always does… He found it! His father laughs, hugs and kisses him. His father's coat smells of bread, it always smells of bread…

Suddenly, he shouted for his wife. He thought for a moment that his wife had returned, that she was home – he heard the clatter of plates in the kitchen and tried to get up, but could not. His body felt very heavy, the scene before his eyes was when he had stood there watching how his wife was leaving the house with their child in her lap. And he thought that his wife's walk was very similar to the one he had seen in the underground crossing. Yes, it was the same walk, the same one…

"Light as a giggle, light as a…" he kept repeating, trying to remember it, to not let it slip away. He had finally managed to accurately describe the walk in the underground crossing. He had forgotten that he had lost his suitcase and, with it, all the walks – his wife's; he had already forgotten his father's. But he was trying to get up from the couch and write his description down on a piece of paper as quickly as possible, so that he would not forget it.

His memory gave him no peace until the very last minute, everything was mixed up in his head, he saw forgotten, disjointed scenes from his childhood and his past, he saw his father, his wife… The images endlessly replaced one another, he heard voices, unintelligible sounds like whispers, he could only understand half of what they were saying but he could not remember it, he thought he heard a child crying, a sound he knew well, he was constantly running, trying to catch up, grab the sound, but failing, he saw how his little, gray suitcase was slipping away from him, and there was nothing he could do, except to shout, "Don't leave me alone!" but no sound would come out.

His last hours were silent and soundless, he was no longer moaning, no longer shouting; at some point he only said, barely audibly, "I smell bread," and he was quiet.

He no longer roams the streets of Yerevan in the afternoon, you cannot see his old pants and dark jacket from a distance anymore. His constantly concerned eyes are no longer watching people walk. Now, as always, Abovyan Street is bustling and, as always, different walks are rushing about. And perhaps, to this day, the small, gray suitcase is sitting somewhere silent and alone, like the life led by the man that owned it…

CROWS

"What's keeping you?" he asked, opening the door midway.

"I'm coming, grandpa," I replied and, picking up the ax, I stepped outside.

We walked down an uneven path, my grandfather walking ahead of me. There were blossoming apricot trees all around us.

"There's going to be a good harvest this year," he said enthusiastically, looking at the trees, "I won't be around tomorrow. You have to come, look around, water the trees…"

I didn't make a sound, he kept talking. We continued walking.

"This is it," he said, pointing to a poplar. We walked up to the tree, "But be careful, don't hurt yourself…"

My grandfather left. I looked at the poplar. It was not very thick, but it was tall. "I'll be done in two hours," I thought to myself, and started to chop at it with the ax.

One hour passed. "I need to take a break," I sat down on a rock and lit a cigarette. I looked up at the sky – crows were circling and cawing noisily. "They've been flying around like that since I started," I noted but, giving it no importance, I finished smoking and continued chopping the tree. After a few blows, my attention was grabbed by a crow that flew down and perched a short distance away. It was not a very big crow; one eye was missing, it moved its thin legs and came closer. I bent over – it had come so close that I could reach out and grab it. I tried to stay as still as possible so that I would not scare it away. I looked into its empty eye socket. "It's probably a chick," I thought. The crow took a few steps, then stopped, looked in my eyes and suddenly lunged at the pack of cigarettes I had left on the ground, and took off. "So I guess he was right," I recalled that my grandfather had always said that crows were thieves and had already stolen several bars of soap from him; I smiled as I watched the bird in flight. It flew up and made a few deft maneuvers before disappearing into the poplar branches and then reappearing in the air a short while later. I noticed that the pack of cigarettes was no longer in its beak. "It must have dropped it off at its nest," I mumbled to myself as I spotted a nest in the middle section of the tree and continued to chop away with enthusiasm, as if punishing the little thief…

The tree fell with a crack. I walked up impatiently, trying to find the nest and check – would the cigarette pack be there? "They might attack me," the thought occurred to me. I looked up at the sky – there were no crows to be seen. I began to examine the nest. A few shards of glass and other useless little items; there was nothing else. Suddenly, I spotted something that looked like a chain. I pulled at it tentatively – it really was a chain, a silver chain, with a small gold, coin-like round pendant…

"What luck!" I rubbed my discovery with my handkerchief. "I wonder if it's really gold."

The round pendant had "Aram" etched into it. I looked at it and tried to imagine him in my mind, and what he must have thought when he noticed that his pendant was missing… "They really are thieves, for sure!" I thought to myself with a smile on my lips and I looked at the sky. It was still empty… I slipped the pendant into my pocket, picked up the ax, and left. I told my grandfather nothing as I stepped into the house, quickly changed into a fresh set of clothes and set off for the railway station. Throughout my time on the train, I thought about the necklace and what it could be worth…

"Mom!" I shouted as I entered the house, and went from room to room. "She must be at the store." I lay down on the sofa and started playing with the pendant. I put it on, twisted it around, constantly examining the writing… I soon tired of this and my eyelids grew heavier and heavier…

"Quiet…" the voice said.

I was behind bars and there were three crows sitting next to each other, a short distance away.

"Be quiet," the crow in the middle shouted again, slamming a gavel on the table several times. "Do you plead guilty?" it asked, looking at me.

I looked around and saw that I was in a large room, crows everywhere…

"Plaintiff, do you plead guilty?" it repeated.

I did not make a sound and kept looking around.

"The court will retire for deliberations on the verdict," the middle crow shouted, angered by my silence, and the three of them left.

The room broke out into noisy conversation. All the crows pushed each other aside as they crowded around the bars. The ones in the back rows jumped up and down to get at least a quick view…

"I bet he wouldn't last for more than two minutes," one of the crows near the bars said to the one next to it.

"You said the same thing about the last one," the second crow replied disdainfully…

Suddenly, a few blows of the gavel were heard and all of them vanished from the area next to the bars and occupied their seats. The three crows were once again sitting at the table.

"Caw! Caw!" the middle one started, looking down at a sheet of paper.

I could not understand a thing. I looked around, as if looking for someone to translate what it was reading out…

"Sentenced to death," it said, ending its long speech. All the crows look in my direction.

"What?" I asked, confused. I thought I had misheard, but the words "sentenced to death" were still ringing in my ears. "I don't understand. What do you want from me?"

"The verdict is not subject to appeal," it replied dispassionately, "Carry out the verdict!"

I did not manage to make a sound, the crows threw themselves at me noisily and I was standing on a chair in the middle of the courtroom, in the next instant, my hands tied. The crows had surrounded me and were waiting… Suddenly, one of them shot up towards the ceiling and attached a rope and noose directly above my head.

"Why?" I screamed in terror, realizing that they were getting ready to hang me, "What have I done?"

"Your last wish?" I heard a voice behind me say, and someone placed the noose around my neck.

"But what have I done?" I screamed helplessly.

"Your last wish!" the voice repeated.

I tried to see who was behind me, but I could not…

"I want a smoke," I said, convinced that crows did not smoke and attempting to make things awkward for them.

"It worked!" I thought, noticing that they were looking at each other in confusion and that none of them came forward.

"Little thief, is that you?" I shouted happily, surprised at seeing the one-eyed crow break through the crowd to rush toward me. It was like seeing an old friend, a feeling that I was saved…

"Am I the thief, or are you?" it said contemptuously as it flew onto my shoulder and held up an open cigarette pack to my mouth. "If you hadn't stolen that pendant, you wouldn't be in this situation now. You can go and die for all I care!"

"No…" I noticed the cigarette pack, "My pack of cigarettes!" I shouted, trying to break free.

One of the crows struck the chair. I felt an unbearable pain around my neck, my body swung in the air, the crows had come closer and watched greedily, as if afraid to blink so that they would not miss a moment.

"I told you he'd barely last two minutes, didn't I? He's going to lose consciousness now," I heard a voice say.

My eyes filled with tears, I could not see well, I was running out of air, it started to grow dark… Someone called out to me in the distance, the voice came closer and closer; it was a voice I knew…

"Mom!" I gasped deeply and shouted, opening my eyes.

I was at home, on the sofa, greedily sucking in air, as my mother looked at me in fear, crying…

"What happened?" I asked, "Mom, what happened?"

"It was tight around you… It had clung tightly to your neck, it was strangling you," she sobbed, pointing at the pendant on the floor, "I barely managed to rip it off…"

I rush into the corridor, my head spinning. I felt weak and looked in the mirror, the pendant had left a mark on my neck, there were spots of blood here and there… My mother watched me and wept, an immense fear in her eyes…

I picked up the pendant from the ground and noticed in horror that the first letters of my name had appeared where "Aram" had previously been. I rushed to the window and threw the curtain aside. I flung the pendant as far away as I could and, right before my eyes, a crow grabbed it in the sky and vanished from view the next instant.

JESUS' CAT

I was in the fifth or sixth grade when I got involved in this story. The teacher and girls weren't in the classroom, and the boys had crowded around one of the seats, laughing. I came closer to find out what had caused such hilarity and saw Narek sitting in the middle of the group, patting a gray cat that was peering fearfully out of a half-open backpack.

"What's going on?" I asked with excitement.

"Someone's tricked Narek and sold him a cat," Tigran replied, with pink eyes that had teared up with laughter.

"Nobody's tricked me," Narek said.

"Someone probably picked it up from the trash," Tigran continued, "And they told him it was Jesus' cat, and he believed them."

"Nobody's tricked me, nobody's tricked me. There is a breed of cat like that, it's very rare. It's called Jesus' cat because it doesn't drown, it can walk on water," his eyes blinked rapidly as he spoke.

A new wave of laughter broke out. I wasn't sure what was going on, but the pervasive laughter was infectious.

"That's what you were told by the person who sold it, right?" Karen jumped it, "You're such a moron."

"…"

"…"

He kept patting the cat and insisting that he had not been tricked, that this breed of cat really could walk on water. Things got to a point where Narek and Karen almost ended up hitting each other, after Karen had reached out to the cat but Narek hadn't let him touch it. They grabbed each other by the collars, but we pulled them apart.

"Idiot, you ripped it," Karen said, running his fingers over his collar, his cheeks covered in tears. "Are you crazy?"

Narek didn't make a sound, he was caressing the cat with his head hung low, as if nothing had happened.

"Hey man, check if Screecher is near the main door," Karen said, turning to Grigor, his green eyes shining with anger.

Screecher was what we called Ms. Adibekyan, one of the vice principals. She'd earned that nickname for her high-pitched voice and her tendency to often speak loudly. She'd stand near the central entrance of the school during the breaks and check to make sure that the children wouldn't slip out.

"She's near the door," Grigor confirmed after he'd returned.

"We'll get out through the bathroom door, then," Karen decided and, looking at Narek, he added, "You're coming too."

It was only when we turned to the street that led down to the gorge that I realized what Karen was thinking. Something told me that I should go back, I didn't want to be a part of what was about to happen, but I was also consumed with curiosity, and turning back halfway would have been awkward – what would the guys think? As I walked, I looked at Narek, tightly holding on with both hands to the yellow backpack, and an image flashed in my mind of his mothers' tired hands…

At the end of every month, an opaque plastic bag would appear at our teacher's table, and everyone would understand that Narek's mother had stopped by. She would never let a holiday go by without expressing her gratitude to our teacher, and the latter knew her job well; during the breaks, from time to time, she would ask Narek to leave the room and she would tell the rest of us,

"When he gets up from his seat during class and walks around the room, or when he does other weird things… ignore all that, pretend that you don't notice it… Narek has a nervous condition, he's getting treatment, this is all temporary, it's nothing serious… We have to help him, but if you laugh or react to each of his actions, then you're making it worse, pretend not to notice."

And she would add, "Not a word of this in Narek's presence" before leaving.

And so, his mother kept visiting from the first grade and personally thanking all the teachers, and I would look at the bulging veins on her hands, reminiscent of the soiled roots of trees, and it would make me sad. What was it about those hands, why did I find them so captivating? On the first day of school in first grade, all of us wore white and stood in the school yard while our teacher, whom we had just met for the first time, told us to stay quiet during the principal's speech. Nobody was listening to what the principal was saying, or perhaps they were. But I remember that I was gazing absently at Tigran's dark purple coat; he stood out from everyone else, like a black pigeon among white doves. While I was taken by the golden buttons on the coat, a thin woman, holding her son by the hand, walked up to us. It was them. Even at that very first meeting, her hands had not escaped my notice, the bulging veins demanding my attention, suggesting something sorrowful in the whole thing…

Tigran and Karen walked ahead of me as the hot wind slipped for a second time over the sweaty back of my neck, and it was only then that I realized how I had kept looking at my feet to predict a possible attack by that treacherous snake. They said that the previous year, when the hot air had hung low in the gorge, and when silence had risen to the sky from the scorched rocks, an amazingly beautiful snake had come out and bitten a boy. He had reached out his hand in an attempt to grab the snake by its head, but the snake had bitten him. Nobody had been down in the gorge that day except for the boy, and by the time his friends had dragged the injured boy out, his hair had turned completely white. The venom had turned his hair white, but his body had fought back, and the boy had been lucky, he had lived…

We walked along the downhill path, and small pebbles slipped out from beneath our feet. I kept imagining the boy with white hair. I would see him every day in the school corridors, he was a grade older than me, and he would no longer go down into the gorge, he would never go down there again…

"It's going to rain for sure," Grigor said to me.

"What makes you say that?"

"My arm is throbbing. When you have a fracture, you become more sensitive to coming rain, the fractured location starts to hurt before it starts. My arm's throbbing now."

"…"

"…"

"…"

"Could he be right, that there's a breed of cat like that?" He asked in a voice that only I could hear.

Grigor didn't ask any more questions. Throughout our walk, he talked about his fractured arm and the coming rain. I wasn't listening, his words slipped out into the air, while my attention was focused on the snake that was hiding somewhere close by. I was scared. When we got to the river, the water reflected the light and seemed to be winking at me, trying to hint that I should go back, that I didn't want to be a part of what was about to happen; but I stayed…

"Nobody tricked you, right? All right, then. Drop the cat in the water," Karen said. "Let's see it walk on water."

Narek didn't make a sound, he stared back and blinked.

"Can't you hear me? Are you deaf? I said, drop it in the water…"

Everything happened quickly – I saw Karen reaching out to grab the backpack, and then it was in the river. The backpack floated on the silvery surface, bobbing up and down as if trying to grab hold of a rock. But the water flowed quickly, very quickly. For a moment, Narek stood immobile, watching the departing backpack as if hypnotized, doing nothing. Perhaps he couldn't believe that he no longer had it, that his fingers had handed them over so easily to someone else, with no resistance. He knew, he had felt that there had been resistance, his fingers had not given up quickly; they hurt now, there was a prickly feeling in his palm, but he was doing nothing… Perhaps he understood well what was going on, perhaps he was simply waiting for something to happen, watching and waiting…

When the backpack was already at such a distance that it looked like just a yellow dot, he regained his senses, as if the fog that had been gathering around him had suddenly disappeared, and he rushed after the bag with teary eyes. I watched as Narek ran along the river's edge, and I saw the hands with veins like soiled roots, they seemed even more sorrowful…

Yesterday morning, when the thought had occurred to me to go to church, I had the most unexpected of meetings. Narek stood there before me, wearing a black vestment all the way down to his shoes. I kept staring at him, I couldn't look away. It had been years and nothing seemed to remain of the Narek I had known. He was tall, wearing glasses with narrow lenses, a thick beard covering his face. I wouldn't have known who he was if he hadn't recognized me and walked up to me. Nobody had seen him after the incident in the gorge. They said that his mother had taken him to a different school… During our brief conversation, I managed to tell him that I had become a writer, that I wrote stories. I don't remember what else I told him, but I remember that I kept saying how good it felt to talk to him, and I kept saying thank you. He smiled and expressed surprise that I was thanking him, but at that moment it felt like a huge burden had fallen off my shoulders, and I was truly grateful.

THE BASEMENT

As far back as I can remember, I've always been with my dad, I spent my whole childhood hurrying after him; he had the habit of walking quickly, as if he was always running late, and I was forced to run late with him. We would go around the city for hours, he would stop by one acquaintance or another to see whether or not one of them had found him some work, while I would wait near the entrance. Once the fruitless search of the day was over, we would go to the basement, where the others were. I've put a lot of thought into trying to come to some kind of an understanding of who the others were, and what it was that united these different people; perhaps it was the only thing that poor people have in abundance – hope. Now, when I try to recall every memory, every detail that has been carefully concealed within me, only one color appears before my eyes – black; those people, the basement and everything else was black, except for the freshly painted orange floor. The basement was huge, with a ceiling that was high, very high, with a window slightly below it, covered by a grill, through which the feet of passers-by were frequently visible. I can't say much about the basement, I remember how Samvel used to say, "We seized it from the rats."

Each of us had our place – I sat in the creaky chair, which was mine alone. Slightly further from me, near the computer, was were Samvel would sit, a man past fifty who was so thin that his cheeks were like bowls, always sunken, and when he crossed his legs it looked like he had only one lower limb. He was an extremely calm man, always speaking in a sleepy voice, with a cigarette permanently dangling between his fingers. He was different from the other members of the basement, he didn't lack any money, they said his wife was rich… Samvel was, so to speak, the "founder and central figure" of the basement, everyone was connected to him in some way and he was a part of everyone's affairs; everyone owed him money, but almost nothing was ever spoken about that. It's difficult to say what the point was of the basement, or of the small change that he would earn during the day by doing tasks for someone or other using the computer, it wasn't like he needed to do any of it… I liked sitting next to him and watching for hours as his fingers deftly flowed along the computer keys, while letters kept appearing on the screen. I didn't understand any of it, but it was interesting, computers seemed like an unachievable dream for me, a completely different world…

To my left, right below the window, was where Ashot Yeranyan would sit. He was a strange man, he never ate meat, he was a vegetarian, and he looked like how Jesus is portrayed in the movies, with blue eyes and light-colored, curly hair. They would say that he was a man of profound faith, and when I asked my father what that meant, he said that such people stood close to Jesus. It was probably that response that triggered the association of his resemblance to Jesus on my part. Ashot Yeranyan was an architect—a "cheap architect", as we would say jokingly—and his table was always full of huge papers, with countless lines crisscrossing and splitting across them. What I knew about him was limited to what he himself would say, but he would barely speak, he was always quiet; sometimes, he would recount his story and say that he and his wife adopted three orphans after the Spitak earthquake, two of whom had disabilities, and they raised them with great difficulty. However, after they sunk into poverty, they were forced to hand the children over to an orphanage. He would tell us how his wife, unable to bear it, had left him, and he—now completely alone—had ended up here, in the basement.

"Why would I need a house?" he would say when I asked him why he left home, and he would add in a whisper, "She suffered a lot with me, I hope she's happy now, the house is a gift from me to her."

It took me a long time to understand the meaning of these words, and to comprehend why he lived in a rented apartment if he owned a house. It was only much later that I understood that his wife had left him and found another man…

Ashot the Box Man sat not too far from the door. He had earned his strange nickname because of his work – he would make boxes for flowers and sell them to flower shops to earn his daily bread. I have no memories of how he dressed and other such details, I only remember his face and the fact that he was short. It is impossible to forget a face like his—anyone who's seen it even once would attest to this—it was so prominent that later when

I tried to recall anything about him, nothing else would come to mind, as if only his face had existed.

"If you had a couple of horns, you would make a perfect Satan," my father would say when he wanted to tease him, "If they knew where to find you, Hollywood producers would line up to offer you parts in their movies."

Ashot the Box Maker would not take offense at these jokes about his appearance. On the contrary, it seemed like he shared this opinion. He was a fiery individual, always on the move, and his shifty eyes and rapid speech emphasized the impression that there was something satanic to him. I would stand next to him sometimes and try to understand how he would take a piece of paper and turn it into a box in a few seconds, it looked easy… Ashot the Box Man owed everyone money. He would borrow money from all of us with the hope that his plans would work out on each occasion; he always had interesting strategies for making millions quickly, but something would always thwart his plans at the last possible moment.

"It's going to work this time, I've thought of everything," he would say each time and he would explain the "ingenious" details of the plan.

Once he had thought of preparing air fresheners for cars, the kind that hang from the rearview mirror. And—you know what?—he did it. He dunked some paper into lemon essence and they started to smell nice. But his invention ended up with unintended side effects – all of us smelled of lemon for about a week, because he had organized his experiments in the basement. The strongest smell naturally came from the experimenter, and it was so strong that he was forced to get by without public transport for a while because he had been thrown out on more than one occasion. He was forced to go from place to place on foot, and tried to avoid staying for long in closed spaces… His family history was also quite confusing; he had a wife and two daughters, but he hadn't seen them in a long time.

"I'd just left the building and the brick fell right on my head," he would say excitedly, "My wife had dropped it, she wanted to kill me, she still does…"

In contrast to Yeranyan, he would talk about the collapse of his family with great enthusiasm and pleasure, and it often seemed like he was making it up because it was so colorful and illustrative. He would constantly repeat how his wife had wanted to kill him because he was unable to make any money, how she had turned his children against him, and so on. Hearing that story, I tried to imagine his wife; I thought that she must have been such a devil to have reduced him to this state. With Samvel's permission, Ashot the Box Man would sleep in the basement, lining up a few chairs next to each other and lying down on them…

The next "resident" of the basement was Opposition Tigran, a man of average height who was always dressed solidly, and I thought he was a writer. He always held a small briefcase full of papers, and he had a notebook with a silver cover in which he took notes when he heard something interesting.

"He's a supporter of Levon," Samvel had said when I'd asked him what "opposition" meant, but that explanation was as vague to me as the word "opposition" itself. I couldn't understand what it was he did, but I thought that he was a very important man because he rarely visited the basement, and when he came it would always lead to something unpleasant.

Once, when we came to the basement as usual, I noticed that the computer was gone. Nothing like that had ever happened before, and I couldn't understand what was going on.

"But why did they take Samo away?" Ashot the Box Man said and laughed to himself, but the others were in no mood for humor. It turned out that the police had come and taken Samvel away by force along with the computer, saying that he was suspected of having anti-government material on the device. Samvel was set free only after the intervention of his wife's relatives, but the computer was not returned to him. It was clear to everyone that Tigran had been involved in some way with the appearance of the police and the confiscation, but as always, he was not there. Opposition Tigran was a die-hard drunk, and he would drink so much that he'd end up in a faraway corner somewhere and then sleep it off. He was often found in dumpsters, but when he didn't have any money, he was an extremely intelligent person and it would never occur to you that he could be a drunk. He would drink down to his last dram, and everyone knew that he had had some success and earned some cash when he disappeared from the scene for a few weeks. Tigran would take money from people who wanted to go abroad and he would register them in his political party, print a few passionate articles in the newspaper about how that person was being persecuted for his political beliefs and so on, and that person would soon be allowed to leave the country. His most recent transaction had also led to the unexpected confiscation, as we later discovered. A few days before the police had come, he had asked Samvel to type up a text that had contained anti-government sentiment… I didn't understand any of this back then, and I didn't really want to understand it either, but I only knew that they were not going to return the computer and that had been enough to make me sad. A short while later, Samvel got a new computer, of course, and it was better than the old one, causing me indescribable joy. Soon, everything was like before, except that Tigran was nowhere to be seen…

The only person who didn't have a permanent place of his own in the basement was my father. He always sat in different spots, as if he couldn't stay in the same chair. When he spoke with excitement, he would always move to another chair, and if there wasn't one available, he would stay on his feet… My father was a painter, and like almost all the artists in Yerevan, he was poor. He earned his daily bread by painting portraits. He would paint portraits of famous Armenians and display them as samples, leaving them with his acquaintances in the hope that someone who wanted a portrait would see them and we would be able to extend our existence for another few months. My father and I constantly walked around the city, we would walk a lot, and he had invented a game to keep us from getting bored. He would say the name of the street where we were located at a given moment and then it would be my turn to name the next one, and the game would go on until one of us was unable to name the street, or made a mistake. He would often lose on purpose to make me happy. My father always had hard candy in his pocket, which he liked a lot; and when he noticed that I was getting tired, he would give me one. He also had another habit. I'd noticed that when we walked past the display windows of cafes or shops, he would always turn his head the other way, as if he couldn't bear to look at the items on display, and when I asked him why he did that, he would smile and say nothing in reply.

All of the memories of my childhood are linked to my father and the basement. Something interesting would always happen that would turn a regular day into a memorable one. My father had once painted a portrait of Charles Aznavour and brought it to the basement.

"What do you think?" he took the portrait out of a plastic bag and leaned it against a wall, asking with pride, "It looks like him, doesn't it?"

It was a beautiful painting, Aznavour smiled kindly at all of us. My father talked about it with enthusiasm, pointing to one part of it, then another, on which he had done a lot of work…

"Sam, it's good, isn't it?" he kept asking, confident that if Samvel liked it, then anyone who had money to spend would like it as well.

Yeranyan and Samvel were awestruck, and I was proud of my father, as if the words of praise about the painting were all being said for my enjoyment. But it all lasted only until Ashot the Box Man appeared.

"So you're such a big fan of the President that you've painted his portrait?" he said when he saw the painting, in the tactless way that was characteristic of how he spoke.

We all laughed, thinking that it was a joke, but Ashot was insistent.

"What are you talking about?" my father then said angrily, finally realizing that he hadn't been joking, "It's Charles, can't you see?"

Ashot had stood near the painting at the time, and hearing what my father said, he began to walk in our direction and after examining the painting carefully from a distance, he laughed and said,

"It looks like Charles from far away, but up close, it's the President."

And that turned out to really be the case. When you stood close to the painting and looked at it, it was the President. But from a distance, it was Charles Aznavour. We were all shocked and kept moving back and forth, as the portrait kept changing before our eyes. My father couldn't explain it,

"Nothing like this has ever happened before," he said with surprise, "What a catastrophe! And I used so much paint on it."

For almost a week, my father tried to erase the President from the portrait – he added wrinkles, changed the skin color and the position of light and shadow, and even painted when drunk, but the President persisted. He would close one of his eyes and stand at a slight distance from the painting, extending his arm and holding his thumb out to cover one section of the painting or another, as if trying to find where the President was hiding.

"Can you believe it? He's already grabbed everything, now he wants my painting too," he would say, half-drunk, "No, I won't give up, I'm going to fight and save my painting."

"Do you think I'll be able to get him out of there?" he would ask me. "Maybe he's very jealous of Charles in real life, yes, that must be it, maybe there are problems between them… Maybe I should paint a self-portrait to see who is jealous of me…"

For a long time, the main topic of discussion in the basement was the painting. Everyone was interested in how things were turning out, and my father would laugh and reply that the President was stubbornly refusing to leave. He kept trying to find an explanation for that strange occurrence, saying that the similarity was in Aznavour's forehead and eyebrows, and up close the face would seem flatter, looking more like the President, so everything made sense.

"It's a two-faced portrait," Ashot the Box Man said during one of the discussions, and that name stuck to the painting – "two-faced."

No matter how much my father tried to erase the President, he couldn't succeed. Eventually, Samvel grew so fond of it that he bought the painting and hung it on a wall in the basement, right above his head.

Time was flying by, and the first hints of fuzz had appeared on my cheeks. It seemed to me like everything was moving around me, changing, except for the basement and our lives. In the basement, the two Ashots were sitting as usual at their desks, Samvel was in his place as well and the "two-faced painting" hung above him, Tigran wasn't there, and I was walking around town, hoping to collect orders for portraits. I had begun to walk around on my own lately, my father was not in good health, walking long distances would tire him. After doing my rounds, I would rush to the basement.

It had rained that day, and the streetlights were already being switched on, there were few passers-by. I was walking carefully to avoid getting my shoes wet. I had almost made it to the basement and was getting ready to enter when I suddenly heard a shout. I recognized it immediately – it was Ashot the Box Man.

"Let me go, let me go," he was shouting.

When I went in, Ashot was on the floor, my father and Yeranyan were trying to calm him down and help him up, but it was in vain, he was resisting, lashing out first at one of them, then the other.

"Leave the room," my father shouted, noticing me.

I couldn't understand what was going on, Ashot was crying and saying things that didn't make sense.

"Let me go, you don't understand, the city is a box, a big box, I've seen it with my own eyes," he shouted, pointing to the window, "Soon you will all be inside it and you'll never ever be able to get out…"

I stood there and didn't know what to do. It was a terrifying scene, he kept repeating endlessly how he had seen that the city was a big box, which kept growing, swallowing everything that stood in its way, and that it was coming after him…

Soon, Samvel returned with paramedics and they took Ashot away. Up to the moment when the ambulance showed up, he had kept resisting stubbornly and repeating the same thing… From that day on, nobody mentioned Ashot in my presence, and when I was in the basement, everyone pretended that nothing had happened.

"Ashot hasn't gone mad, no, the city is truly murderous," I heard my father say once, when I was eavesdropping.

A short time later, the basement was closed off to us. Samvel had not paid the rent, saying that he had found a better place, but the truth was that it had become impossible to stay in the basement, everything reminded us of Ashot.

There is still a structure curled up behind the buildings on Abovyan Street, containing the basement where we once gathered. A dentist's clinic has replaced the basement and nothing remains from the past, but I always have a strange feeling when I walk past it. An inexplicable and powerful force always makes me stop for a moment, as if that spot has the ability to freeze one's glance on the spot. But there was nothing like that really, of course, the basement exists for me alone, only I can see it…

I often roam around the city now, in keeping with habit, and start at Abovyan street, then walk down to the Opera… The streets come up one after the other, crisscrossing and splitting beneath my feet, as I pass the same spots where I once walked with my father, where I spent my childhood, and I often feel like my father is with me, at my side… Now I know why he kept turning away from the display windows, why he said that the city was murderous… I roam around the city unhurriedly, turning my eyes away from the display windows of shops fearing—fearing immensely—that I'll turn back and see that the pink buildings of the city have been replaced by a gigantic box, rushing towards me.

ADADA

The voices are shouting, the voices are silent,
the voices lead to a dance with the devils,
an absurd scene before God…

I cannot decide whether my eyes are open or not, whether it is dark; I try to move my limbs, they are numb and prickly. "Where am I?" It's like I am in a closed space. "Perhaps I'm in a room?" I feel the ground with my hands, it seems like I'm on soil. "Where am I?"

"Smoke?" I hear a voice ask.

"Who is it?" I ask despite myself.

I'm scared. "So I'm not alone, whose voice was that?" I'm very scared, I can't see a thing.

"Who are you?" I ask again.

"Smoke?" I hear again, after a short pause.

"Who are you?" I shout, "Who are you? Tell me at once, otherwise… So, you're laughing, are you? Who are you, you son of a….

"I shouldn't have started swearing, that was a mistake. What an idiot I am!" I'm scared, it's like he or she is everywhere. I'm trying to remember whether it was a male voice or female, but I can't. "Why have my limbs gone numb?"

"Of course they're numb. You've been here a few hours already," the voice says.

"A few hours? How did I end up here?" I ask, trying to get some information. "Why are you quiet? I'm talking to you…"

"Wait, wait. If the voice said you've been here for several hours, that means he or she was here before you," I heard a new voice say.

"Who are *you*? Who are you people? Where am I?" I shout, "Say something."

"I need to check whether my eyes are open or closed. Perhaps these people have blindfolded me." I don't even know who I'm talking about but I think they are bad people. I run my hands along my face, my eyes are not blindfolded. "My eyes are open, then it must be dark." I try to mentally recall the direction from which the sound was coming earlier, but I cannot.

"Smoke?" I hear the first voice again, I don't reply. "Maybe I'm actually in a room, but how did I end up here?" My head starts to ache.

"What do you want from me, old man?" I scream out those very words.

"Why did I say old man? Perhaps he is an old man, that's what his voice sounds like." I try to recall the voice, but cannot. "Yes, he really is an old man – a thin, tall old man with a wrinkled nose, no teeth in his mouth, just one remaining – the front one, and it's grown so long that when he closes his mouth half of it sticks out between his lips, a disgusting, yellow tooth…" A shiver goes down my spine, the old man does not make a sound. There is silence, just a weak ringing in my head and an irregular heartbeat reflecting in my temples. My limbs are no longer numb. "I have to quickly figure out where I am and why it's so dark here."

"Smoke?" It's the old man's voice again.

"You again? I'm not talking to you," I reply, "Also, I know who you are. You're that old man with the disgusting yellow tooth."

"What about the other one?" he quickly asks, "The one who spoke to you after me?"

"He's right. I guessed who he was, what about the second one?"

"Hey, second one, who are you?" I shout, "I don't get it. Is this the latest thing, a tense silence? I couldn't care less if you never spoke again."

I push against my back; I'm leaning against something hard. "It's probably a wall." I feel around with my hands – yes, it's a wall. "I'm in a room, yes, a room. Or perhaps I'm in a large space somewhere, like a field, and there's just one wall, and that's the wall I'm leaning against or I'm tied to." I move my body around quickly and nothing restrains me. "That's lucky, I'm not tied." "No, if I were in a field, I would be able to see the stars. You can always see the stars, but you can't see anything here. It's a room, in any case, maybe it's in the middle of a field, but it's a room." I mumble to myself and, picking up small stones from the ground, I throw them in various directions. None of the stones I throw make a sound, "so it's a very large room." I try to carefully get up and I'm able to do this without any problems. I raise a hand to try and figure out the height of the ceiling. It's high, my hand doesn't touch anything. I feel something protruding from the wall, it's round, cold, I want to turn it and it seems like I do, I can hear voices again, someone is calling out my name, but none of it sticks in my mind. I immediately release it and sit down on the ground. The voices depart and I feel that I would have moved ahead fearlessly if not for those two. I'm more afraid of the old man, there's something terrifying in his voice but it is also familiar to me, as if I've heard that voice in the past…

"Why aren't you saying anything, huh?" I shout, "I'm talking to you!"

"Perhaps they're waiting for me to come closer, perhaps they're tied up." It is very humid; my body is burning beneath my clothes.

"Smoke?" the old man's voice again.

"What are you, a broken record? Smoke, smoke? I'm sick of your 'smoke', can't you say anything else?"

There is no reply. "Perhaps that was a bit rude." I feel my throat going dry and the taste of resin on my lips. "The thought of smoking didn't cross my mind a little while ago, but now…" Someone calls out my name again, I have to listen hard this time. I strain my ears, I listen, but I can't recall any of it.

"What's going on?" I shout helplessly, sweat pours down my forehead, I'm burning up…

"Do you have an adada in you?" the old man asks unexpectedly.

"What's an atada?" the unfamiliar word seems amusing to me.

"Not atada. Adada," he replies angrily, as if I had offended him by not knowing what the word means. But he continues after a brief pause, "There's a very dark corner inside me, with a chair placed in it. Someone is always sitting on that chair, someone very small and short. I cannot see his face, just his legs – they're chained to the chair, which is why he can't move. He's Adada."

"What does he do when he sits there?" I ask with interest.

"Sometimes, as if at particular times, he says 'adada' and bad thoughts flood my brain, very bad thoughts."

He says "adada" with such enthusiasm that I'm unable to suppress my laughter.

"Why are you laughing? It's the truth. Take today, for example. I was walking past a building and I saw the cover of a coffin leaning against a wall. At that very moment, I heard it inside me – adada. And that was immediately followed by the thought 'Good thing he's dead. That's what he deserves.' I mean, I don't know anyone in that building, I could not possibly know the person who had died."

"What are you talking about?" I shout, "Is this some kind of delusion? Oh God, what's happening to me?"

"It's always like that," the old man continued, his voice trembling, "Against my wall, all kinds of bad, terrifying thoughts come to me. It's not me, though, it's Adada, it's not my fault… I don't know what to do. I can't bear it any more, I feel like wishing evil on everyone, even… even… God."

"Shut up, that's enough…" I cover my ears and scream.

"I'm afraid that he'll break free of those chains one day, I'm so afraid…" he continues, as if he hasn't heard me.

"Enough, you stupid old man, enough!" I shout as loudly as my strength permits, and he falls silent.

"Personal God, personal Go…" a new voice is heard saying after a long pause.

I fail to say anything before another voice can be heard, then many of them. They mix up, I can't hear a single coherent piece, I only manage to capture disjointed sentences and words.

"Men are blind for a whole life…"

"He opened the window and jumped out, flew over the city and fell into an aquarium…"

"Who said that in the world of fear…"

All the voices in the room, all the voices born out of the darkness flood my head, it's unbearable, I press my hands against my head, they won't come out. My heart starts beating rapidly, I feel like the old man's face has come close to mine, very close, he's going to stick his long, yellow tooth into my eye any moment now and I don't know whether my eyes are open or closed… I feel like my eye will turn yellow when he sticks his tooth into it, I can feel his breath on my forehead, I shout as loudly as the air in my lungs permits, I barely make a sound, I try to shout again, I feel a powerful light… "Is it light now?" My eyes adjust to the light in a moment as it wasn't dark a few seconds ago. I look around quickly, it's a very small room, there's nobody there but me. It's a light gray room, there are no windows, there's nothing, it's empty. I get up quickly.

"That's lucky, it's a good thing I'm alone," I say, then start to walk around and explore. The room is around fifteen paces long and six paces wide, my head starts to spin.

"A door?" I mumble to myself and walk up quickly to a door that has appeared before me. I look at it, but I can't recall its shape or color, "It's strange that I hadn't seen this earlier." I notice something, it looks like writing. I bring my head closer – a sharp instrument has been used to untidily scrawl, "Open this door, you will see the devil and God, and then you will die."

"Interesting," I say as I rub my chin and carefully bring my ear closer; I can't hear a thing. I walk away from the door and start to pace in circles in the room, gradually walking faster, "devil, God, you will die" the words keep changing their order but they spin around in my head, and I try to spin in the direction opposite to the words. I notice footprints on the ground, the ground is fully covered in muddy footprints, as if a whole army has walked past before me. "That gives me some hope, but I'm still scared," I laugh.

"I have to find it, I have to find it," I repeat as I pace in circles.

"What are you looking for?" I hear a voice. It's a new voice, one that seemed to come from inside my head.

"Who are you? Who are you? Tell me!" I shout in surprise and look around.

I don't know what to say, my limbs hurt, the voice does not reply, the silence is killing me. "But what *am* I looking for?" I start to pace around again; the room spins faster than me. I try to understand what I'm looking for, my eyes come to a stop.

"Got it!" I walk up to the door and I see my reflection in the shiny, golden knob. I cannot remember what I look like, I put my hand on it, it is cold. "No, not now," I go and squat in a corner. I look up at the ceiling, "I wonder where the light is coming from?" I get up quickly and look in every nook and cranny but there is no source of light. But is it bright. I curl up in a corner again to try and get warm, my body is frozen.

"Where are you, old man? Where are you people?" I scream. There is no sound, it's cold, I remember the old man's voice, I want to smoke.

"Why didn't I take him up on the offer?" I weep, holding my head. I look at the door, "Why not open it? I'm going to die of hunger anyway. At least I'll get to see the devil and God." I don't move from my spot. The words "you will die" are stuck in my head, the knob is tempting, I want to come closer… I get up and walk around to take my mind off it. "Two, three… no it's unbearable. It would be better to die," I reach for the doorknob.

"What? Where's the knob? It was here a moment ago!" I am taken by surprise and look around. "Did I pull it off?" I search my pockets. "What happened?" I say and start swearing out of a sense of being powerless, "Give me back the doorknob…"

I can't make a sound. I walk up and read the writing again.

"Please open the door," I hit it, "Open up, I don't care what happens…"

There's a black gap where the doorknob used to be, it's the size of my eye. "I wonder what there is on the other side," I bring my head closer carefully, "It's an eye, a gray eye, it's looking at me, they're watching me…" I cringe and shiver with fear. "I wonder who it was?" My heart starts to beat faster, I remember the writing, "Was that God, or the devil? Probably the devil, God's eyes would have been blue, yes, it must have been the devil," I start to cry.

"Why didn't I open it earlier? I'm such an idiot, idiot…" I strike myself on the head, "I'm going to die of hunger now."

"Oh God…" I can't take my hands off my head, they're stuck there.

"Release them, release them," I try to get my hands free by moving sharply, but it's like someone is holding them and pressing them against my head… I notice that the doorknob is back in place. "I have to hurry, I have to… Before it disappears again…" I somehow manage to get my hands free and run. The doorknob is cold. I turn it, "It's open…"

The door opens, I'm standing far away, I'm too scared to come close. My heart is beating so hard it's like it's about to explode… The words "God, devil, you will die" keep spinning in my head…

"A mirror?" I say and touch it with my fingers.

There's a mirror behind the door, a large mirror, nothing else. I touch it and look at myself.

"They tricked me… tricked me," I shout with tears in my eyes. I raise my hands to strike the mirror, and suddenly my reflection smiles and says, "Adada."

"Who are you? What do you want from me?" I cringe and scream. "What does all this mean? What have I done? Leave me alone, leave me alone…"

The room goes dark, and I heard a voice close by, very close to my ear, "Smoke?"

ABOUT THE CLOUDS

When you are walking along a street, you never know who will find you. Avoid puddles, you've been so lost in thought you've already forgotten your own address… Cross the street with your hands in your pockets, you are searching for the truth, but the city is too small for what you seek. All you'll find in the city is crows and fear… Be careful, take care of yourself…

The space welcomed me with apples that had fallen around the trees and wet leaves. I looked at the trees ecstatically, it felt like they knew me, they knew whose grandson I was. Every time I went out to that plot of land, I remembered my grandfather because he was the one who built the house and planted all the trees. That land was my world now, my last spot of refuge, where I tended to the apple trees, but more than half their yield had fallen to the ground… Having finished the work, I leaned the plow against a wall and walked into the house to make apple tea. Have you ever had apple tea? I invented it. You take the sourest apples and cut them up into small pieces in a teapot. It tastes heavenly! I sat there in the chair drinking some and looking up at the sad rows of power lines on the blond hillsides. It was getting dark, stars the size of my fist were visible in the sky, you can't see stars like that in the city… After two more large cups of tea, I put on some warm clothes and continued to watch. Barking could be heard in the distance from various directions, and then the signal from the electric train cut through the silence several times, but the departing sound of its iron wheels once again covered me in a wave of numbness. I listened with my eyes closed to the sound of the apples falling… I walked into the house, but I was no longer sleepy. A tree branch rubbed against one of the windows, like someone tapping with his index finger. Nothing was visible outside, the wind was growing stronger, the tin on the roof trembled. In order to stop hearing the sounds of the falling apples, I picked a book at random from the bookshelf and started leafing through it. A fly was doing loops in the room, distracting me. It was one of the big ones, and it was stubborn. It was clearly not the type that gave up easily, I kept missing when I tried to hit it. I thought about shaking the towel in the air constantly, until the fly ran out of strength and settled down somewhere. It worked; I ended our stand-off with a single blow... The fly looked like it had turned into a birthmark on the wall, a smiling birthmark. Nothing more happened, it had been completely immobilized. I looked at it and wondered – life probably treated us the same way too, it pushes us around, forces all our strength to run out, and then deals the final blow. I tenderly wrapped the fly up in a paper napkin and placed it between the pages of the book...

The night went by like a flash, the sun was already rising but I was still thinking about the fly. The impression that there was something similar between us was not giving me any peace. I looked at the pink spot on the wall – the last trace of the fly left in this world. I had to drive these thoughts out of my head, so I stepped outside, the cold morning air was pleasant. Mornings on that piece of land were special, each one was different. There were only a few apples left on the ground, although they had kept falling throughout the night. I quickly gathered up the apples and rushed to make some tea. The trees were happy that I was there... I sat in front of the house and drank it in sips, watching each movement around me. The little insects had woken up and were hurrying somewhere without noticing me. The sky was drowned in blue, slipping by as it scratched against the messily assembled antennas on my neighbors' houses. I looked and thought, how wonderful that I don't have a television or an antenna. My eyes settled on the roof – the pointy top of the triangle had faded and gone black, while the bottom remained red. I vowed not to paint it – looking out from the heights of the train station, you could immediately spot it, like a blossomed poppy. Nothing slipped past my eye, no movement escaped my gaze – I noticed when the cat appeared on the fence and spotted me. As part of our tradition, we had some ham together. I caressed its neck, I had gotten used to its presence. For all these months, it had been my only visitor... The cat stubbornly kept jumping, trying to catch the lizard on the wall and it seemed like it could succeed at any moment it chose, but it was putting on a show for my benefit. It would take a break from time to time to see whether it was having the intended effect on its audience. I watched, unable to conceal my joy. It kept jumping up and down while the lizard remained immobile, as if the two of them really did have a deal…

I put on my shoes and rushed to the water before setting off on the road. I can't say why I always go to get water first before I leave that piece of land. It's like I would have an unlucky day if I did not drink water or look at the stone. Little pebbles rolled away from my feet, the path took a sharp turn and the tap appeared. The water joyfully gurgled and winked at me through the light that it reflected. My grandfather would tell me there was a time when there was no stone or no tap. A man named Artush had installed it in memory of his son who died in Karabakh. I wiped my mouth with my sleeve and looked at the stone while it looked back at me. I continued walking as the shadows of the trees slipped across my face as I walked to the station while eating blackberries… The station was not crowded, you could count the number of people there on the fingers of your hand. I cast a glance at my house again – from this vantage point, it really did look like a blossomed poppy. I sat down on the bench placed at the wall. Twenty minutes had gone by but the electric train had not shown up, although it had been even later on occasion before. In order to avoid boredom, I started to imagine who else had sat on the bench before me. I tried to recreate their features, the color of their eyes, thinking about what they liked to eat, or what other preferences they had. The image that appeared was a gray character, a dark man. His cold eyes looked back at me through his watery lenses, and he wore a broad-rimmed hat from the past century on his head. He sat with a briefcase on his knees, the kind of briefcase that professors carried. He glanced at the time every second or so, bringing his wrist up to his face so close that it touched his glasses. It seemed like the man had not come here to go somewhere, there was another reason. It felt like he was waiting for someone to return, waiting for a long time, getting angrier every minute… New people had appeared at the station, with overloaded bags in their hands – they were taking apples home. Lost in thought, I had not noticed when they had come. I looked them over – many of them were elderly people. Suddenly, my attention was grabbed by a couple that was holding hands and walking in my direction – a mother and her son. The boy walked while looking upward at his mother's face.

"Mom, do you see the clouds when you look at me?" he asked.

The woman was not surprised by the question, as if this was not the first time she had heard it. She replied that she did not. The boy held out an index finger and pointed above his mother's head.

"Then why do I see them when I look at you?"

Then the signal of the electric train could be heard, it was getting closer, it was time to leave, but I kept staring at the clouds…

FEATHERS

The sharp, piercing metallic sound cut through the humid night and entered my room like needles. The sweat-drenched bedsheet had stuck to my body, becoming a second body over my own, and between the two bodies flowed blond, sunburnt dreams as the sound stubbornly poured into my ears and yanked me out of myself. I walked up to the window from time to time and pushed the curtain aside to take a look; the sound repeated, interspersed with brief intervals, and came from the direction of the playground.

It could be heard for so many nights, starting at late hours and not stopping until sunrise. It was clear that somebody was using the rusty swing, but who? Why would anyone need to? All my efforts to spot the person were in vain. That section of the playground was not well-lit, nothing could be seen at night and, when morning came, the playground was deserted. The suspense grew unbearable. At first, I vowed to wait it out, expecting my neighbors' nervous systems to be more sensitive and reach breaking point before mine. But the sound kept ringing out and I got the impression that I was the only one it bothered in the whole neighborhood, that only I could hear it. It was impossible to wait any longer, someone had to put an end to this. So, the next time the sound rang out, I rushed to the playground. As I walked down the stairs, there was a fear in my heart that there would be a drunk or homeless person on the swing. I was sure he would be alone. What was I going to do? I wasn't looking to get into a fight, after all. And what if he had a knife, I thought to myself. Nevertheless, something was pushing me forward.

He sat there in the swing, moving up and down, swimming in the coming dawn. There wasn't enough light to see well, I sensed the movement and could barely make out the outline of his body. I tried to guess whether it could be someone I knew. I had come closer and stood just a few paces away from him when he suddenly realized my presence, scrambled off the swing and fled. It was through the way his body was shaped and how it moved that I realized it was a man. Everything happened quickly and instantaneously; surprised by this turn of events, I returned home. He thought I was going to hurt him, I must have really scared him if he ran away in such a state of panic, I thought. The stranger's movements had left the impression that they did not match his body, it was like they belonged to someone else. I put it all down to alcohol and decided that he was a drunk. Satisfied with myself and the successful conclusion to the task I had set myself, I went to bed. Less than an hour later, I could hear the sound again.

It did not give me any peace for several more days, but I did not dare leave the house anymore. I would walk up to the windows and purposefully slam the panes hard, but to no avail. I was filled with anger at the man and my rage gnawed at my brain. I don't know what would have happened if, one morning when the sky was already blue, I had not noticed that the man on the swing was actually Artak… I had completely forgotten about him, as if he had never existed. But he did exist, and he did not allow himself to be forgotten…

All my memories of Artak are recollections from childhood. He was a year older than me. It would not be right to say that we were friends. Having friends had been a luxury for me during childhood as well. I would play football with the boys in the yard of our building, and he would be there too. I would always take up a position at the goal post, I managed well as a goalkeeper. He was an attacker, he played well. He moved as quickly with the ball as he did without it. It made me jealous that I wasn't as agile as he was, that I was stuck at the goal. I remember one day when the other boys were not around, it was just the two of us. After the game, when I came home in my dusty clothes, my father, who had been standing at the window, called me over and said something strange. He told me to be careful, to avoid getting too close to Artak. I sensed that my father was trying to be as delicate as possible when choosing his words, he did not want to scare me. He repeated that I should play only with the other boys. I found out later from my mother that Artak was sick, she said that there was something wrong with his head from birth, that his father had told my father. I did not understand what was wrong with him and my parents' concern only fanned the flames of my curiosity. Whenever I managed to avoid being watched by them, I spent my time with Artak, examining him carefully, trying to pinpoint his disease, but it stubbornly refused to show itself. I would look at his head every time, certain that the dense growth of hair covered up a network of scars, scars as thick as caterpillars.

All my efforts to discover his disease were in vain. There was nothing unusual about him, nothing set him apart from the other boys. But, over time, something amazing happened. The years went by, but Artak did not grow up. It was like time did not notice him; it was passing him by. Only his body would grow. What happened? Perhaps an important cell in his head refused to be like the other important cells, and did not wish to be a part of what had been decided for it, what the majority had dictated. Perhaps it refused to be afraid of constantly being alone—of tomorrow, of time—and exploded? The boys in the yard and I had other interests now, but he kept playing football, kicking the ball around with children that were seven or eight years younger than he was.

Time flew by. I got into university, and every time I came home from class, I could not help but glance at the playground. It was difficult not to notice that tall man, his face covered with hair, playing with puerile excitement, surrounded by children that could barely reach his waist…

When did he disappear from my sight and how did he come back? I was finding it difficult to answer this question. I had a vague recollection of one of our neighbors once saying that the residents of the building had complained and were worried about the children. They were concerned that he could end up hurting them; he was infantile in his thinking, after all, and you never know whether he could end up getting too excited during a game and losing control. That was why they had taken him to a special institution for people with mental disabilities…

Artak existed and he refused to let himself be forgotten. There was an elusive feeling within me that I had to meet him. This inexplicable feeling rushed me on, as if time was running out. I decided to go down to the playground again as soon as I heard the sound the next time. I thought of taking something to eat with me; I'd read in a book somewhere that an American psychologist had used food to establish contact with one of his patients. Before walking up to the swing, I would shout and say that I was bringing food, then he would not run away. The sound rang out late at night and everything repeated itself like the other night. But even I was very surprised when the idea to take food with me worked. As soon as I shouted about the food, he stopped. He quickly gobbled the apples I had brought; I couldn't see him do it, but I heard it all. I sensed his movement – his body had grown fatter, he was heavy, nothing remained of his previous body. I also sensed that his head hung low, his gaze was averted, he could not look up in my direction…

Every night, when I heard the sound of the swing, I would pick up some apples and rush out in his direction. I would talk to him, ask him if he remembered me, how we had played football together, how I'd always been the goalkeeper and been jealous of his quick moves, of how he could move as fast with the ball as without it, while I stood rooted to the goalpost. He would eat an apple in silence. I tried to get him to say something, but why I did this I do not know. He spoke soon enough… I tried to understand him, to find some coherence in the things he was saying. But the words did not stick together, the meaning they held would vanish at the last instant, evaporating into thin air. I was certain that he was talking to himself, he was not answering my questions, it was like he could not even hear them. On the last day we met, I turned out to be wrong. Artak was sitting on the swing, there was a pigeon in his hand, I could see a white spot in the darkness, and he caressed the pigeon and talked to it.

"When your feathers fell off, you could no longer fly. My father said that you were sick. Then your feathers grew again and you flew off. I saw it, I had been hiding and saw you fly off. My father said you had recovered… You have to fly so that you can live, a bird must fly in order to live…"

You probably weren't there that day, I wasn't there either. They say that dawn had just broken when the residents were woken by the sound of a man crying. People had rushed to their windows to see what was going on. There were feathers outside, like snow. But they had not fallen like snow, they had lazily risen up from the ground, swaying. A man was on his knees, weeping, striking his hands against his head, his son was dead. They said that the pigeon feathers were everywhere, he had stuffed them into his pants, his shirt, his shoes, and jumped off the building. Nobody knew why Artak had done this, all they recalled was that you could barely see the man through the large number of feathers in the air… People said all kinds of things; they felt very sorry for Artak—more so for his father—and they talked. I later found out that the residents had indeed complained at one point, but Artak had not been taken to an institution, his father had not been able to come to terms with that option. Instead, he had created a new world on the roof of the building, out of everyone's sight, and he had kept pigeons there so that his son would not get bored…

People said all kinds of things. But nobody talks about Artak now, they only remember him when they see the man with the stooped shoulders and the premature white hair. They feel very sorry for Artak, more so for his father… There are nights now when I hear the sound of the swing; I know the swing is empty and there is nobody on the playground, but I hear it. It's like he's calling out, sliding through the blind shadows of the buildings, stubbornly pouring into my ears and yanking me out of myself. And when the sky grows blue, the sound is silenced… Everything ends when the sky grows blue…

MACINTOSH

The story started in the winter, when I was a reporter for one of the city newspapers and the editor-in-chief gave me an assignment to write a story about a homeless person. The editor was in two minds at first – perhaps this assignment was too difficult for me, would I be able to deliver? But, with stubbornness that is characteristic of me, I would have none of it, I assured him that I would do a good job. He took his time to explain the complications and nuances of the task, saying that I had to pick some-one as the hero of my story who was at the bottom of the social ladder while managing to retain his or her humanity, so that we could pull at the emotional strings of our readers. The editor repeated the word "emotion" several times, after which we said goodbye and I left the office, and it was only then that I realized the confusion that was weighing on my shoulders. In the bus, throughout the journey home, I was pondering the fact that I needed to find a homeless person with a story that would tug at the heartstrings of our readers – but how could I find such a person? I had two weeks to write the story, but I set about finding a hero for my piece the very next day. The thought of going to one of the spots frequented by homeless people struck fear into my heart – I had always avoided those people, and tried to quickly walk past when I saw them on the street. "The smell that comes from them is disgusting, not to mention the fact that they could infect you with all kinds of diseases during a brief conversation," I thought. After hesitating for a long time and thinking twice, I decided to go, there was no other way.

I put on the most ordinary clothes possible and picked up a journalist's most important tool – my recorder, and then I rushed to Mashtots Avenue. I thought that I would have no problem finding one of them near the Opera building, I had spotted them around there before. But after half an hour of walking around, I realized that it was pointless. There was nobody there.

Perhaps I had picked the wrong time, or the significant police presence was the issue. I decided to call an old acquaintance, Tigran, with whom I had grown up in the same neighborhood. He was now an alcoholic, happy to spend time with anyone as long as it meant a free drink. He had told me once how he had sat down for a drink with the local homeless people. He heard me request that I wanted him to introduce me to his "friends" and he heartily agreed to help.

"I'll introduce you to Grandpa Yura. He lives a couple of blocks down from us, in that five-story building… But bring some vodka with you… Don't forget the vodka…"

I bought the vodka and met my acquaintance at the agreed time and place. We were going up the stairs of the building and I was surprised at the idea that this homeless person lived in an apartment. When we got to the fifth floor, where his apartment was supposedly located, the thick iron door befuddled me even more. Tigran rang the doorbell and a very old man appeared in the doorway a few seconds later. His body was firm and his back straight, his old age betrayed only by his white hair and beard that had gone yellow around the mouth because he smoked.

"What's up?" he asked.

"We've come to pay you a visit, we want to sit down and talk a bit," my acquaintance said, and we walked into the apartment.

As I settled into a chair in the kitchen, my shock hit a new level. Out host took out some smoked ham, cheese, and canned food from the kitchen, setting the table for us quickly. Trying to maintain control over myself, I took out the vodka I had brought, and we drank a toast to making each other's acquaintance. I waited until the old man left the kitchen before I attacked Tigran.

"Is this some kind of joke? I told you I needed a homeless person, and you've brought me here to this retired gentleman."

"This is where the homeless people gather every evening. Calm down and be patient…"

As we talked, I discovered that Grandpa Yura did indeed organize gatherings at his place every evening to make up for his solitude and to give him something interesting to which he could look forward. But not every homeless person had the right to come into his place; the door would open only to those who were well-behaved and looked after themselves to some extent. My acquaintance told me that the old man would give them food, drink with them, and even let them spent the night on occasion. He had never had a shortage of visitors.

"Mug and Karo are coming," our host said when he came back, and we continued to drink.

Grandpa Yura told me that he used to work at the lamp factory, that he had four children and ten grandchildren. He said his children were well-off and did not need anything; he did not meddle in their lives, and they did not meddle in his. While the old man told me his story, two gray figures joined us. They were Mug and Karo. Once I saw Mug's facial expression, it wasn't difficult to guess how he had gotten his nickname. He frowned down on the table, and emptied glass after glass without making a peep. Karo was more outgoing, we began to talk immediately after we were introduced. When he found out that I was a journalist and that I was going to write a piece about one of them for the paper, he grew excited; this seemed to be of interest to him.

One toast followed the other and, as at any other gathering of men, once we had downed a few shots we began talking about women, which is where another surprise lay in wait for me.

"I'm softer than before these days, I'm not the same," Grandpa Yura said, putting a cigarette in his mouth, "I can barely manage being with a woman two or three times a week."

"How old are you? I thought that, once a man hits sixty, he no longer can…"

"Of course I can, and how! My Angel will be hear any minute now, you can ask her… I'm going to be seventy-three soon, but I have no complaints when it comes to my health."

Angel arrived not much later. She was a thin woman past forty, with a body that was still attractive. She looked better than I expected, it was only the slight puffiness of her face and the variety of clothing on her body that hinted at her belonging to the lower rungs of society. Our host introduced us and, opening the bottle of suspicious vodka that Angel had brought with her, he filled our glasses, and it started all over again.

The old man was in a good mood now, he was joking around, pinching Angel. I felt that the time had come for me to leave, and all I needed was a good moment to make my move, which arrived soon enough.

"We're leaving. When the old man is with a woman, he doesn't like to see us hanging around," Karo said, adding with a smirk, "Let's leave these youngsters to themselves and go upstairs. You can see how we live."

When we left the apartment, Tigran and Mug said they had some things to do and left, while I stayed with Karo. He opened the door to the roof and started going up the stairs.

"Scared?" He asked, laughing. "Nobody's going to touch you, we're harmless people."

"It's not people that scare me, it's rats," I confessed, walking up carefully.

"There are hardly any left, we've poisoned them all…"

We walked, overturning some boxes, scrap metal and other junk that was underfoot. Even though he had said that there were no rats left, I kept expecting one to lunge at my feet at any moment. Indeed, not long after that, a long, gray form detached itself from the corner and rushed across my feet. A shiver ran down my spine, but it turned out to be a cat. Karo put an amicable hand on my shoulder, suggesting that I should keep walking and not be afraid. Soon, I could hear a song. I thought I was imagining it, but the closer we got, the more audible it grew. "You are Armenia…" a female voice sang cheerfully.

Walking around yet another box, we finally got to our destination and, seeing myself in the "living room," I froze. My expectations of people living on the roof of a building were that I would see countless empty bottles, the remains of food scavenged from trash cans, and there the homeless people would be, in the center of that smell and garbage. But the first thing that caught my eye when I walked in, was the television placed on a small wooden stand. The television was working; I was so taken by what I had seen that I did not notice the man sitting in the corner near the furnace, and it was only his warm hello that brought me to my senses.

"This is Macintosh," Karo introduced us and we shook hands.

My new acquaintance was a tall, thin man past fifty, whose facial features and clothing made it difficult to believe that he was homeless. He was clean-shaven with a sharp nose and thin lips that suggested nobility. His gray eyes held a cold, peaceful gaze, and the image was completed by a long, light-gray trench coat that reached down to his calves. I looked at him and could not make sense of it. He seemed like someone who had a government job or something… While I sat there examining how he looked, Karo joined a few boxes together to make a table, took out a bottle of vodka—which he had apparently swiped from the old man's table—and continued where we had left off…

That was how my visits began. Every day, I would buy some sausages and vodka, then rush to the roof, where they would be expecting me. We would set the table and start to drink, while I would try to extract any information that would be useful to me. But I only managed to have conversations with Karo. The other two were kind of reserved while Karo, on the contrary, would talk all the time, recalling all the stories that were going through his head. It seemed like he was making up a large part of it, there was something artificial in the things he was saying. It was not difficult to guess what he was trying to do. He was obviously saying things that he thought I wanted to hear in the hope that I would end up writing the article about him. I would press the record button and watch the show.

"I've been to all kinds of places," he said, "I've even been to Kamchatka… Then I turned into a hippy. I'm not in touch with any of those guys anymore, though, they're not the same – they have families and stuff. But you know what kinds of things we did back then? Remember when they'd put up a huge picture of Brezhnev near the Opera but someone had poured paint on it at night and run away? Who do you think was behind that?"

"I'm an anarchist at heart, I'm against any kind of government. I don't care whether it's the Soviets or the anti-Soviets – I'm against all of them. I'm always against everyone… The Communists would catch the homeless people and force them to work. Who cares about us now? The government doesn't even notice us now, for which I would say a warm, 'homeless' thank you to them…"

"Nobody wants to accept what I'm saying—nobody would like to admit that the city has turned into a pile of trash—but if you were to walk around Yerevan one day and notice that it was perfectly clean, do you know what would happen to you? You would be terrified, you'd lose your mind, thinking that all the people had vanished…"

Karo took pride in the fact that he had never worked for the state in his life, not for a single minute, that he was the freest and most independent person, and many other things. When I asked how he survived—he had to find something to eat every day, after all—he said that there was always money available not just for something to eat, but for something to drink as well. There turned out to be many ways to make money – emptying trucks or bottles at the market, collecting scrap metal and handing it in for recycling…

With each passing day, his stories grew more and more imaginative. Following Karo's contagious example, Mug also started joining in the conversations and the only one who refused to communicate was Macintosh. He would sit unnoticed near the furnace, listening to us carefully, but he would not say a word. The neat way he dressed and his elegant movements had shocked me when we had first met, while his withdrawn and reserved nature made me even more curious about him. I would press the record button and watch his every move out of the corner of my eye. I had noticed that he was the only one who did not drink at all. He would take his share of the food and withdraw into the corner. There were many other things also worth noting in Macintosh's behavior that had not slipped past my eye. But the most impressive of these was how he would take out a pad from his breast pocket from time to time and make notes based on our conversations. What was he writing? Why was he doing this? On yet another occasion when we had come together on the rooftop and had already emptied a few glasses, we started talking about women again. Karo was asking me if I was with anyone, why I wasn't married and so on. I responded to all those questions by saying—I don't know why I chose these words, they just slipped out—that my wife was on her way. When I said these words, they seemed to grab Macintosh's attention; he immediately took out his notepad and wrote something down…

It turned out that there was an interesting story to how Macintosh had ended up on the roof among homeless people. They said he used to live in Belarus, but nobody knew what his work had been. He had ended up in Armenia because of the books he wrote. Nobody had seen any manuscript, but the word was that he had written about chess and football. Mug told me with excitement, as if through the eyes of a witness, that the books were educational guides. When they had refused to publish them in Belarus, considering them ahead of their time, he had gone to Russia, hoping to get them published there. He faced rejection in Russia too, and the publisher there advised Macintosh to try in his homeland, so he had come to Armenia… The books had never been published, he had run out of money, and it had been three years that he had "ended up stuck."

"He told me all this," he added, "They're about chess and football… For example, this is the kind of thing he would write about – when the ball is coming down from a certain height at the goalkeeper, should he watch the ball, look at the attacking players, or…"

The conversation was active in Macintosh's absence, but the only clear piece of information that I managed to extract was that he got the nickname Macintosh because of the gray trench coat he wore.

The things that Karo and Mug were saying seemed too primitive to be credible. I was very suspicious; I had an inner feeling that there was something important I had not been told… When Karo and I were alone, I turned out to be right. He confirmed that Macintosh had been in Armenia for three years and had been unable to leave. He did not reject the other information that I had, but he added that Macintosh had a wife and two daughters, who were still in Belarus.

"Don't you think the woman has a bigger role in this whole story? Don't be naïve – whatever's happened has happened because of his wife… They've banished him from home and said get out and get by any way you can…"

"Has Macintosh told you this?"

"Nobody's told me this. You'd have to be stupid to not see it yourself…"

He insisted that he was right and tried to convince me that the root of all of Macintosh's troubles was his wife.

"Why hasn't she tried to find her husband in all these years? She's in Belarus, her own country, she probably has family there, nobody's been holding her there against her will, how much money does a plane ticket cost? Why couldn't she have bought her husband one in all this time?"

True to habit, Karo spoke a lot on that day too. He said that Macintosh worked as a bouncer for a restaurant somewhere. He didn't get much of a salary, but he never went hungry. He had been writing letters to government officials over the past three years, asking for help to buy a ticket and so on. In the end, he took me to a section of the roof that was separated by a tablecloth… Surprisingly, Macintosh's "room" was very different from the rest of the roof. The floor was painted, there was light purple wallpaper on the walls, and there was a bed on the ground. I noticed that the ends of a pair of pants were sticking out from beneath the mattress. When I asked what that was for, Karo laughed.

"This is how we iron our pants!"

Everything that Karo had told me made sense, but knowing his personality, I was inclined to consider all of it a figment of his fertile imagination. Was Macintosh's wife really behind all this? Perhaps he *had* been banished from home… These questions and doubts multiplied after the unexpected incident that occurred next.

Grandpa Yura showed up and Karo was praising him, recalling how he had allowed them to live on the roof, when Macintosh appeared and told us that he was leaving. It turned out that one of the letters he had written had finally succeeded, he had found a sponsor… He stood in the middle of the space – no suitcase, no bag. All that he owned was on his person – the long trench coat and the faultless pants. He walked up to each of us and said goodbye. When it was my turn, he squeezed my hand and smiled, adding,

"My wife is on her way."

It was the first time that I saw him smiling…

We saw Macintosh off, and then started to drink. I walked around alone for a long time after that. I don't know whether it was the weather or the alcohol, but the feeling of being incomplete that always pursues me when I walk the streets seemed somehow to have doubled. I felt like something was missing, something important… I got home around midnight that night. As soon as I walked in, I sat down at my desk. Everything that I had recorded or noted lay there in front of me… I picked up a pen and wrote down the title – "My Wife is on Her Way."

MEETING

To Gurgen Khanjyan

I cross the street and direct my steps to the neurologist's house. I've not been feeling well lately; I can't listen to anything anyone says; every little sound gets on my nerves. It's like everyone is shouting, I can't watch television, I don't feel like seeing anyone. I've isolated myself – I don't leave the house, I don't even switch on the lights at my place, light hurts my eyes. I sit all day alone at home in the dark.

The neurologist's elder daughter opens the door, greets me warmly and tells me to wait in the living room. I say hello to the two men sitting there, take a seat on the greenish couch in the corner, and wait. I hang my head, I'm picking at my nails, and it feels like the men can't help but stare at me. I peek out of the corner of my eye – no one is looking at me. I know one of them, I've seen him several times, he's one of my neurologist's patients, but I'm seeing the second one for the first time, although I can tell from his face that he's not a nice person. The daughter reappears soon and says that her father is ready to see me. I already know where I need to go, I open his door and say hello as I walk in. The doctor is seated in his regular place, behind a small table. I take a seat in front of him.

"Well, how are you?" he asks coldly. I don't make a sound. "Go right back home and take this medicine," he takes out a gray box from a drawer and puts it on the table, "This is the strongest medicine available; if this doesn't help you, nothing will."

I take the box and leave. Throughout the way back, I try to make sense of what the doctor said. There's a fear in my heart; I can guess what he was trying to say, but I stubbornly want to fool myself into thinking otherwise. I reach home and when I enter, I spot myself in the mirror. I look terrible, my eyes are tired and red, I haven't shaven in such a long time that it looks like I'm planning to grow a beard. I enter the kitchen and open the gray box. There's just one pill in it, a medium-sized white pill. I fill a glass with water and prepare to swallow the pill, but a strange fear holds me back, even though the best professional in the city had advised me to take this medication. Also, the information printed on the box is in a strange language. "It would probably be better to break the tablet in two and take just half a dose," I think and carefully make two pieces of it. I quickly throw one piece down my throat, swallow it down with water, and I tenderly place the second half on a plate before going to the living room to lie down on the couch. Half an hour has gone by and I feel no change; I cannot even imagine what change I should expect, and I stare up at the cracks in the ceiling, the only pastime that has not yet bored me. I realize that nothing has changed and I decide to take the second half of the pill as well; I am about to get off the couch when one of the cracks in the ceiling starts to move. I leap out of my spot, my heart racing, and I look carefully at the ceiling, but it seems like nothing is moving. "I imagined it," I mutter to myself, and turn to move toward the kitchen, but then suddenly notice that the crack is moving again – this time, it slides across and stops in the other corner of the ceiling. The surprising thing is that the crack does not stretch into the corner of the ceiling – it slides across like a crafty little creature. My head starts to spin and I notice that several other cracks are moving, and then all of them start to move together, quickly, quickly, as if playing a game, trying to catch each other. Without thinking, I rush out of the house, and go down to the yard; I don't know what to do, but I can't go back, the cracks are there. I have nowhere to go. I stand outside for a few minutes but then realize that it is cold, so I decide to go to the church; I recall that the church had a gas connection installed recently, so it must be warm there, and it is just a short distance away. My head spinning, I don't stop, quickly rushing up the uneven path to the church entrance, where I walk inside. There's nobody there, some candles are burning in each corner, I look around hoping to see someone, but there's no one. I walk up to a bench and sit down.

"I haven't been to church in a long time," I study the church ceiling and the paintings hanging from its walls, trying to see if they had added anything new. Besides a huge tunnel, which is exactly where the altar used to be, everything is the same as before. At the very center of the church, or rather, in its deep corner, where the altar with the red curtains used to be, there are now two huge arches—one on the right wall, the other on the left—and these passages are connected to each other by a railway track that is visible on the ground. It's like I'm standing at the Yeritasardakan metro station, except that the space for the tracks is not as long. I look at the arch on the right, and then on the left – it's dark and I can't see anything. I think that it's one large tunnel, except that this one part of it is open so that people can get on board, like at a metro station. There's a cold wind blowing. I stand there a little while longer, but then feel inexplicably disappointed and go back to sit down in my previous spot. It gets colder and I'm starting to shiver, when a man suddenly walks up—as silently as possible, as if not wishing to be noticed—and sits down next to me.

"Sit down, I'll stand," I give up my seat to the stranger, even though there's nobody else in the church except the two of us and all the other benches are empty.

"Thank you, this is where I always sit," he replies with a smile, "Why are you barefoot?"

I look at my feet and I am indeed barefoot. I try to explain myself to the stranger but I cannot, and a strange feeling comes over me, like I'm embarrassed or put down.

"Take these, put them on," he takes his yellowish slippers off his feet and says lovingly, "We're going to walk, I don't want you to get cold."

I quickly put on the slippers and follow him. He says something, I don't quite catch it, it's like he isn't talking to me, but I know for sure that he is addressing me. I want to say something to him and try to put my words together in a way that is decent and educated, but I can't. The stranger is very ordinary in his speech, he seems to make no effort. We're walking and he's talking, I'm constantly nodding as if I understand, but the meaning of his words slips by me at the very last instant. I look at his face. "I wonder where he knows me from, where have we met?" No, I am unable to remember. His face keeps changing…

"Do you want to die?" he suddenly asks. It's not the question that throws me off, it's more the fact that I've understood him. Ever since we started walking, these were the first of his words that I comprehended.

"I don't," I reply.

"But you don't want to live either," he says and continues to walk.

It is only then I notice that a bicycle is going past us and a little boy is running behind it; there's nobody sitting on the bike but it is moving, constantly making circles around us, and the little boy wants to catch up with it, but is always one step behind. The stranger stops and so do I. We look and it seems to me for a moment that the boy is me, my childhood self. It's boring, the same thing constantly repeating, the bicycle rolling in circles and the boy trying to catch up with it, in vain. I don't understand why we have stopped. I can no longer resist, I hold out an arm and grab the bicycle, the boy stops.

"Take it," I say, "Take it and stop playing here; this is a church, not a playground."

The boy doesn't take the bicycle, he takes a few steps back and starts to cry. "Perhaps I was a bit harsh," I try to placate him. It's no use, his voice keeps getting louder.

"What's wrong? Didn't you want to reach the bicycle?"

"I did," he replies and starts sobbing even louder. His cries ring out across the church and I feel embarrassed, as if he is my child or a family member. For some reason, I feel responsible for him. I give him the bike angrily.

"What should I do now?" he looks into my eyes and asks, taking the bicycle in fear.

I don't understand the boy, he is waiting for my response, then he puts down the bike and sits, starting to weep quietly. There is an oppressive silence, the boy's question keeps ringing in my ears; it is a question I know well, but I have no answer. I turn towards the stranger who is standing a short distance away; perhaps he knows what to do? He walks over unhurriedly, puts a hand on the boy's shoulder, takes the bicycle and pushes it. It starts to roll about in circles again and the boy grows happy, wiping his tears away with his fists, he starts to run after it…

The icons on the walls of the church shudder, as if in an earthquake, and the light from the candles flutters, a train appears. It stops, the doors open, and I realize that the stranger and I are sitting on the church bench, the same place we were before I had noticed the boy, as if we had not walked or moved from our spots. I want to walk and examine the train from closer up. I take off the slippers and return them to him with thanks, only then noticing that his feet were wounded and bleeding. The stranger puts on the slippers, but his blood has frightened me and I try to leave quickly. As if sensing this, he gets up from his place, and tells me that the choice is mine, that what I want the most is time, and then he leaves. I don't understand anything he said and quickly glance at my feet to see if there's any blood on them, but there isn't even a trace. Remembering the train, I quickly walk up to it, but all the seats are taken. I try to find a free spot and suddenly notice someone waving at me. I strain to see and realize that it's my neurologist, he's pointing to the seat next to him to indicate that it's free. This makes me happy but before I can get on board, I realize that he's gesturing and trying to explain something to me. I understand that he is asking about the medication. It is only then that I recall the drug and the crawling cracks on my ceiling. Despite myself, I nod to indicate that I have taken the pill. He responds with a gesture to suggest that I should get on the train, then he sits down again, seeming relieved. I hesitate and recall that I had taken only half the pill and I feel awkward about lying. I think about running home, taking the second half and then rushing back. I notice that the doctor has walked up to the window and is looking at me questioningly. I signal that I will be back in a minute and start to run as fast as I can. I open the church door and start to feel a mild headache, which grows stronger. I don't stop, I keep running, raising a hand to my forehead. It's moist and I think that it must be sweat, but when I wipe it off, my hand is bloody. I'm scared, my heart is racing, the walls start to clear. "I'm home," I look around and I am truly home, but the floor is wet with blood from my forehead. I try to stop; it is difficult but I succeed. I go to the bathroom – the wound is not a big one, and the blood has clotted. I can't remember anything; all I can recall is that I took half the pill. I think that I must have had a reaction to the drug and lost consciousness, there is no other explanation. I pull myself together, my dizzy spell is almost over, and I feel relatively better. I go to the kitchen and glance at the window. It is dark outside. I look at my watch – I've been unconscious for around five hours; the second half of the pill is on the plate. Angry, I pick up the phone and dial the number… No answer… I call again… Finally, a woman picks up the phone and tells me that the neurologist died suddenly a short while ago. I hang up…

BIRDS IN THE SKY

He was like my little shadow, constantly hovering around me, studying my every step and move, and when we ended up standing next to each other, he would gaze silently into my eyes and smile. There was an inexplicable sorrow in that smile, as if he was asking for forgiveness, trying to explain…

He was probably eight or nine years old, it was difficult to tell his age because of his build – he was short, but had a large head, swollen like a balloon, which distracted us from any attempts to guess how old he was. Who was he and where had he come from? I kept asking him questions in Armenian, Russian, and broken English, trying to guess his ethnicity. It was all in vain. He would patiently listen and smile quietly. Nobody knew anything about him, we didn't even know his name. Kamil, a few of the other boys and I—the ones that knew Russian—had named him Medvezhonok, or little bear. We had not picked that name randomly – the way he moved and walked was truly reminiscent of a bear, and he was like a little cub. His legs—curved like pieces of wood that bend in humidity—took each step with what seemed like extreme lethargy; he seemed to be so lazy in his movements that we assumed he would never leave his bed if not for the urges to eat and go to the bathroom. He would spend part of the day lying down, his face always turned to a wall. Every time I walked past him, I threw a glance in his direction, wondering if he was asleep. But I had never caught him sleeping, he was always awake. As soon as he spotted me, his eyes would shimmer like ripe blackberries and he would smile that same apologetic smile… How did he not get bored, staring at the same blank wall? What was he thinking, was he thinking at all? When he wasn't in bed, he would follow me around like a shadow – he did not do this with anybody else, only me. I thought, perhaps he is mute and keeps following me to let me know that he's Armenian too; but there was another Armenian boy there besides me – Hayk from Georgia, and the two of us would often speak in Armenian. He would never follow

Hayk, only me. Everyone called him Medvezhonok, even the foreigners who didn't know what the word meant. He had grown accustomed to this new name and would respond when called. Sometimes, the boys would point to an empty glass, letting him know that they were asking for some water, and then they would watch him shuffle off like an inflatable boat to fulfill their request. They would guffaw and shout "Medvezhonok", mocking the way he moved. He would smile in response and continue his crooked shuffle, as if he were walking through a thick layer of snow, his legs barely able to advance…

Kamil, Hayk and I spent most of the day together and he would be by our side. Silently, without making a sound, he would follow our conversation, as if he understood what we were saying. As soon as I glanced in his direction, he would smile and his thin, mulberry-colored lips would reveal small teeth, huddled around each other. Kamil was a year younger than me; he was eleven – an energetic boy from Ukraine of medium height, with blond hair and eyebrows. Every night, when we prepared to go to bed, his torment would set off; he would constantly roll about in bed, trying to pull the covers over his face. Kamil's hands were ruined, he had no fingers, an ugly mass of flesh stood in their place. He had told us that a friend had pushed him when they were playing, and he had fallen hands-first onto an electricity fuse box. He said he had been lucky to survive. Hayk was exactly two months older than I was. He was from Tbilisi, but spoke Armenian fluently. He said he had harelip, half his upper lip was missing, and his teeth were in two rows—like a shark's—triangular and sharp, very sharp… Every time he smiled, he instinctively raised his hand to his mouth, ashamed…

The huge room, which used to be a basketball court, was full of more than two dozen children with disabilities. The beds lined up near the walls held children without limbs, boys with burn scars that covered their whole bodies. The Afghans were the ones in the worst condition – with lifeless limbs, hardened jaws and faces. The long, milk-colored robes the Afghan children wore gave them an air of mystery, especially at night. I would lie in my bed and watch them rush to the bathroom in turn; they were like ghosts floating through the darkness… Here, we had no parents, religion or homeland. The only thing that united us was disease, we were all unwell… When it was time to sleep and all the lights were switched off, there was only a single bulb burning in the corridor, the light from which would slip into the room through the crack in the doorway, cutting through the darkness in the room like a broad-bladed knife. At that time, one could hear dull sobbing, some of the children pulling the covers over their heads as they cried, others feeling no need to conceal their weakness. And soon, everyone would be weeping, as if crying was contagious…

I would have the same dream every night. My faded memory would bring the wallpaper from a wall in our house before my eyes. I would not see my parents or anything else, just the wallpaper. I would touch the wall with my hands and run my fingers over the protruding pattern… It was so real, so close…

Our connection to the outside world was the glass door that was always closed, and the small window that was just slightly lower than the ceiling, which meant that you had to climb to the head of the two-level bunk bed to reach it. The Afghan boys managed to reach the window with surprising ease, bunching around it in groups of three, opening it and gazing in wonder. What could they see? What was on the other side? Mountains? A forest, perhaps? Could it be the sea? Their eyes were so awestruck, so shiny, it was as if they were absorbing the outside world, afraid to look away for a second in order not to miss any of it. They would wave and whistle, as if calling to someone… During the day, the door would open several times at scheduled hours, and people with medical masks would walk into the room. They would come in twos and threes, once they had even been a group of five. They wore white gloves, they were doctors. They would take instruments out of their silver suitcases, examining each of us, then taking notes in a pad, and leaving. None of us had any idea what they were writing, none of us knew German and so we could not ask. Even if there had been a German speaker among us, he would probably not have dared pose the question. The masked men looked frightening – one of them wore rings on one brow, the other had an arm covered fully in tattoos, they were like billiard balls or smiling skulls. They would examine everyone except for Medvezhonok. Every time it would be his turn, the masked men would look at their list and then leave without examining him. On one occasion, one of the masked men had even affectionately patted his nearly-hairless head…

The very first day we arrived, we were all given badges that had a blue frame; we were made to understand that we should never lose ours and always wear it on our chest. They did not have our first or last name on them, just a bunch of numbers and some other unintelligible writing, probably information about us. We were each assigned a number; I was thirteen. I would often examine the paper, turn it this way and that, sliding my eyes over the letters in the Roman script, but they meant nothing to me. The badge had a picture of a boy and a girl holding hands, it was probably their logo. Something interesting happened one morning. The day was just starting, most of us were still asleep when a siren sounded. One of the boys—thin, with a face that had cracks like a melon peel—walked up to his compatriots and woke them up, saying something, his voice not concealing his panic and concern. Soon, all the Afghans were on their feet, walking up to us in confusion and trying to tell us something, perhaps seeking to ask us for information. It turned out that the boy had decided to make some noise after he had woken up and found the bed next to his empty – his friend was not there, one of the Afghan boys was missing… No matter how hard I tried to remember the face of the lost boy, I could not. They all looked the same to me. Nobody had seen or heard anything, the boy seemed to have vanished into thin air. They said he had been in bed before the lights went out, so whatever had happened must have happened at night. Hayk insisted that the masked men must have been involved, Kamil and I agreed. But it was unclear how they had managed to come in without anyone noticing. Had we all been sleeping so soundly? The Afghan boys were restless, they kept pacing from one corner of the room to the other, infecting us with their concern. We were all worried that the unexpected disappearance would not be the last one, that it would happen again, and the same fate would befall each and every one of us. The fear that the masked men could return at night kept us all in a state of expectation, and the closer it got to bedtime, the greater our anxiety grew. Kamil, Hayk and I vowed to stay awake and sound the alarm in case we noticed anything. When the lights went out, we realized that many others had thought along the same lines as us – the darkness in the room kept filling and growing heavier with whispers, everyone was muttering to their neighbors… Kamil was saying that he was going to ride a bike from dawn till dusk once his hands were cured; he said that his father had promised to buy a bicycle if he recovered and returned home… It had always been like that. When there was nothing else to say, they would tell each other about what they planned to do once they were well. One of the Georgian boys would limp over each time and say something in Georgian;

I would not understand a thing, but he would talk so enthusiastically that I would nod despite myself, not wanting to offend him. One day when I asked Hayk what that kid wanted from me, he replied that the boy thought I was a Georgian, and had been telling me about what he was going to do once he recovered. He was also asking whether I wanted to undergo surgery soon like him, so that I would get better. I asked Hayk to tell him that I did not speak a word of Georgian, but it didn't help. He would come over again and talk to me with the same excitement, and I would keep nodding my head…

Kamil talked about bicycles through the night, telling me which ones were good, which ones were not quite up to the mark, and what to do if one part or the other broke down. Hayk and I listened without making a sound, perhaps because our fathers had never promised us bicycles… Dawn had long broken when I was shaken awake by an unexpected sound. The Afghan boys had once again gathered in the middle of the room and were shouting, hopping around… Why were they making such a noise? Had somebody been taken again? I looked around in fear, checking to see if everyone was in place – Kamil and Hayk were in bed, rubbing their bleary eyes. We hadn't managed to hold out after all, we had all fallen asleep… The Afghans grew in number, more and more of them leaped out of bed and joined the group, pushing each other around, each one of them trying to break through the crowd and get closer to the center, like ants gathering around something sweet. It turned out that the ruckus was not because someone had disappeared, quite the contrary. The boy who had vanished the previous night was standing in the middle of the crowd. He was dressed in new clothes from top to bottom, his hair neatly combed, and he was wearing blue sneakers – it was only his swarthy face that betrayed his Afghan origins. His compatriots had surrounded him and were looking him over, touching his jeans, putting their hands in his pockets, running their fingers on his colorful t-shirt… That day the Afghans celebrated, they didn't let the boy sit still for a minute, they kept asking questions, and listened carefully when he replied… The boy had a bandage on one elbow.

One day, when the door opened again and the masked men appeared once more, to our surprise, they brought in small and large boxes instead of the usual silver suitcases. They brought in a television and cassette player. The appearance of the television should have changed our daily routines, especially given that they had also brought several dozen cassettes of cartoons. But several of the Afghan boys continued to stand on the bed and stare out the window. Only once did they approach the television around which we were sitting, casting a curious glance at the new item in the room, before going back up the bed. The desire to reach up to the window kept growing stronger and stronger inside me, it would probably not be difficult to climb up to end of the bed, especially with my height. But I was afraid that I would get into a scuffle if I tried to go up there, someone would push me or pull at my leg, and I would end up falling… I was gesturing for them to tell me what they saw on the other side of the window, what filled them with awe, who they were waving to… The only person who neither went up to the window nor came to watch television was the thin Afghan whose shoulders were always hunched. He was a head taller than all of us, they said he was older. His jaws and knees barely functioned, he would rarely stand up. When eating fruit, he would rapidly rub it against his teeth like a toothbrush, and swallow the pieces only when they had been reduced to a watery mass… He loved apples very much… He would spend most of the day sitting alone in front of the glass door…

That day, the men walked into our room without masks, they were smiling at us. One of them began to read a paper he was holding and anyone whose name was read out would be escorted out of the room. When the Afghans heard their names, they leaped for joy.

"Grego…"

My name sounded heavy and alien to me, and I did not respond at once, as if it had not been me. This was not the first time I had heard it pronounced that way, the Germans had always said "Grego" instead of "Grigor", I was used to it. But it sounded alien nonetheless… A few Afghans and I were accompanied down a long corridor that connected our room to the glass door. There were prosthetic limbs attached to the walls of the corridor, while one wall was fully covered with photographs featuring smiling adults who had been cured. I knew the spots occupied by each photograph without looking – the black man photographed near the Statue of Liberty was on the right, third photo from the bottom, the man with the orange cap was in the middle… Kamil said that they had been here once, like us…

The bathroom was a large space that was divided into two by a partition; there were showerheads lined up along one wall. The person accompanying us gestured for us to take off our clothes and enter… The warm water slid down my neck, twisting like a snake, as I rubbed the shampoo into my hair and kept looking back to see if there was anyone there. The Afghans were at the other end of the wall, splashing water on each other and laughing shrilly… I wanted to finish quickly and step outside; I was embarrassed and didn't want anyone to see me naked, although we were all in the same situation once we had taken off our clothes… I was mostly embarrassed because the person accompanying us was still there… When I turned around yet again, Medvezhonok was standing there in front of me, a blue towel in his hands, looking me in the eyes and smiling… I was taken aback and wanted to say something—I don't know what—but when my eyes automatically slid down his small and plump body, the words stuck in my throat. Between Medvezhonok's legs, there was a tumor the size of a fist, like a balloon filled with blood… So that's why he walked that way, that's why the masked men never examined him in our presence… Medvezhonok was smiling…

As soon as we stepped outside the bathroom, the Afghan boys and I were given new clothes to wear; it had all been planned in advance, the clothes fit us perfectly, there was a boomerang on the yellow t-shirt I was now wearing… The glass door opened, we were accompanied out and the paved street that stretched into the distance, was full of children of various ethnicities. Some were in wheelchairs, others had casts on their arms or legs… One black child saw our confused little group and—perhaps as a sign of greeting, or just a random act—raised his crutch, shouted something and started waving it happily… Our quarantine had ended. I walked around cautiously, as if searching for someone I knew… Where were they taking us, what was going to happen next? I tried not to fall behind the person accompanying us as the image of Medvezhonok grew denser before my eyes and the tumor was right before my eyes, the blood in it growing darker… Suddenly, I noticed the building, with a window visible just below the roof, some arms sticking out of it. I recognized them at once. It was the Afghan boys, crowded on the bed as always, looking out the window. Following their awestruck gaze, I saw a flock of birds flying in the sky, they were so beautiful… so beautiful…

SELFIE WITH A TEAPOT

When I wake up now, I can't decide whether I've slept a day, a week, or a month, and my sense of space is fluid – I'm neither inside nor out. Lying in bed all day, I stare up at the cracks in the ceiling and listen to the sound of the trees scraping against the window. All that matters is not giving up and looking at the walls. As soon as you look at the walls, that's it, it's over. I clearly understand what will happen if I look at the walls and I wake up every morning full of determination not to do this, come what may, but my eyes slide to them despite myself and start yet another journey from the door through the walls and the windows to the other side. The secret is in the wallpaper; every time my eyes end up looking at that snow-white wallpaper, they are fixated to it, its pattern sets a trap and manages to exert an inexplicable control over my will power. Soon, there are scenes floating in front of my eyes that I thought I had long forgotten in the depths of my childhood, that I believed were left behind in a place thousands of kilometers away, or perhaps never happened… And I look at the wall, and it will start any moment now, the pattern will grow more prominent, the room will crumple up like a ball of useless paper, small like my fist. Everything is too real to be an illusion, and I feel like I can touch the objects if I hold out my hand, the image absorbs my body…

It is the sunniest day of my life, the rays penetrating through the window and the curtains have cast a pattern on the table and me. I'm sitting and looking at the ripe, red pieces of watermelon, and my mother comes and goes, telling me to take my time eating, saying that I wouldn't have to go. I really want to eat some, but the thought that I would then need to go to the bathroom on the plane holds me back, and I keep asking my mother whether or not she thought I would have to go… Outside the window, it is astoundingly sunny. I try to distract myself by placing my forehead on the window and staring out into the yard – several boys are riding bicycles, and I try to remain as hidden as possible because I don't want them to notice me. The bicycles constantly race from one end to the other. Suddenly, a black spot appears on the street; I don't recognize it at once, and only after it takes a few steps do I realize that it is my father. There is something different about his gait and the way he moves, he has his hands on his back and is walking unhurriedly, as if each step he takes is being met with resistance, he is fighting time, trying to stop it or step beyond its realm. It feels like my father is smaller, his arms and legs are shorter, he has no neck at all…

"You know, I had a dream about you," I say.

"What kind of dream?" he asks in a disappointed voice.

"I dreamed that you were sitting alone in a church pew, talking to yourself. At first, I thought you were praying, but then I realized that you were talking to yourself. You were wearing yellow slippers." He looks at me with a broken smile and grows smaller. I go on, "I was riding my bicycle after that, or rather, I was running after it; there was nobody on the bicycle, it was going on its own."

"When your arm gets better, I'll buy you one. When you're back, I'll buy you a bicycle," he grows smaller still.

I decide not to say anything else, so that he does not grow any smaller. Instead, he speaks,

"By the time your arm gets better, I'll be done with that painting. I can't go to the balcony now, it's like it's looking at me…"

I remember the painting my father had left unfinished. Every time he's tried to finish it, I've broken an arm. I go to the balcony and stand near the incomplete composition. The flowers—as big as my head—look back at me and sway. I've never seen flowers like these before, I wonder what kind of flowers they are. My father stands next to me and looks at the painting. He's so small now that we're the same height.

"The saddest thing in life is to die," he looks at the painting and adds after a pause, "Those who believe that are truly lucky."

I leave him alone with the painting and step in from the balcony. I walk up to the window, the sundrenched street is empty, the boys are gone. Suddenly, my uncle's silver car parks in the yard.

"…"

"…"

"No, he's not going to Germany, I'm going to treat my boy to a meal, we're going to eat and drink, aren't we?" My uncle says and smiles at me…

"…"

"What about the watermelon? You wanted some, didn't you? Eat some before you leave…" My mother says, standing confused in the doorway, and her eyes look so green, the kind of green that covers the hillsides after the rain, I've seen it once. I look at my mother's eyes as they grow distant and try to retain that image. But it shifts quickly, and the scene changes, I'm in Germany…

It rains first, then it's sunny, then it rains again. The weather changes so often, so quickly, that it is impossible to adapt. I'm with the Afghan whose jaw and knees are barely functional, we sit in front of the glass door for most of the day, watching the weather change. In those rare moments when the rays of the sun flood the little yard that lies in front of us, I am constantly full of conviction that the sun in Armenia is different. It's like the sun here is weaker somehow, pale, unable to burn. The one in Armenia is different; it can peel off the skin on your forehead and nose, flood your eyes, making them burn until it pours out of them with your tears. It's feeble here. I wonder what the sun is like in Afghanistan and I look at the Afghan, trying to guess. When I'm not near the door, I'm walking in the corridor, examining the photographs and prosthetic limbs that line the walls. The most interesting thing, however, is the bulletin board, which has colorful pieces of paper attached to it, and there is writing on the papers. Kamil says that they were made by the children who had been here before us, leaving us with their well wishes upon their departure. He shows me one of the papers and explains its contents, he's already translated three papers for me. Everyone's found their papers, mine is the only one missing. I search for it angrily, my eyes looking for Armenian letters; I have to look more carefully, it has to be there… I think I found it. On the bottom of one of the papers, there are some words in small, barely legible writing, "I'm the son of a farmer, I have the hands of a farmer." Weeping joyfully, I read it over and over, the tears burning my cheeks. It's a good thing nobody can see me, everyone's asleep, it's just me and the Afghan in the corridor. He doesn't notice me, he's sitting near the door and staring outside, but it's dark out. I read the writing several more times, then pick up a pen and write in big, Armenian letters next to it, "I'm the son of a painter, I have the eyes of a painter…" The image shifts again…

There are large, blue plastic bags attached to the walls so that the Afghans could spit in them, but they keep spitting on the floor. They stand next to the plastic bags and demonstratively spit on the floor. They have a sort of rebellious, obstinate personality. They're always restless, unable to sit quietly in one place, running around, shouting, hot-blooded. They won't calm down until they break something. Kamil can't stand them, he keeps saying that they're stupid. Every time he talks to one of them, he swears or uses a mocking name while he addresses them with a smile. Perhaps the Afghans did the same with us, but this act of his amuses us every time. We look and find ourselves unable to resist laughing, but he does not. Here's Kamil walking into the room now. He's run around so much that his blond hair is sweaty, the strands clinging to each other, like drenched ears of wheat. I don't look at his hair, it's his hands that grab my attention – they're like blossomed roses, without any fingers, he finds it hard to wipe off his sweat. He says something to me rapidly, he's always in a hurry, his blue eyes constantly moving… The lights in the room go out, we lie down in our beds, Kamil and I are on the upper beds of two-level bunks, close to each other. He tries to pull the bedsheet over his face, but cannot, then tries to slip under it, squirming like a worm, but that doesn't work either.

"Stop it, let me sleep," I shout, angry at the creaking bed.

"I can't, my hands…" he replies and starts to sob. There is anger and powerlessness in his voice…

Kamil and I cry all night, I want to say I'm sorry, but I can't… It's almost morning.

"Kamil, do you dream of home, of your parents?" He doesn't reply, he's still mad at me. I continue, "I've been seeing the same dream for several nights now. My aunt's husband waves at me from afar, there are churches with lofty domes around him. We don't have such tall churches in my country, I've never seen them. I waste no time and run to him, the sky-blue Zhiguli my aunt's husband drives is parked in the square surrounded by the churches. The huge square is empty, and it feels like the colors have turned to stone in this universal silence. He opens the back door of the car and, a smile on his face, looks to one side. There is something important waiting for me inside. I leap towards the car at once and, once inside, I see the wallpaper we have at home. The car is completely covered on the inside with the wallpaper from home. I run my fingers over the pattern, caressing the white surface, my aunt's husband keeps smiling…

"…"

"…"

"What are you going to do once your hands are cured?" I ask him, staring at the streak of light stretching across the ceiling. "Kamil? What are you going to do?"

"I'm going to ride my bike, all day, morning till night time," he replies with excitement, "What about you?"

"Me too," the light from the ceiling blurs as tears fill my eyes once again…

The smell of iodine wafts in from the corridor, the masked men have brought some bread with butter and jam. I take my portion and rush to my bed so that I can eat in peace, but then I hear a voice behind me,

"Grigor-*gori, gori*-Grigor, Grigor-*gori*…"

It's the Uzbek boys – ever since they found out my name, they've been shouting it whenever they see me. They are both covered in large burn scars, the skin on various parts of their body looks like a wrinkled sheet.

"Why is your name the same as the Russian word for 'mountains'?" they ask.

"It's not."

"Grigor-*gori. Gori* is Russian for mountains."

"My name has nothing to do with mountains," I say.

"Grigor-*gori, gori*-Grigor…"

I leave the bathroom and put on my new clothes, then walk to the bulletin board to look at that paper for the last time before my departure. I cannot find my writing, nor the one that had been there next to it. Instead, I see another text in Armenian – "They took me out of Germany, but they cannot take Germany out of me…" The door is open and we leave one after the other, the yard is full of children. The Afghan boy, as always, is at his spot near the door, staring with a cold gaze after everyone leaving. When his eyes slip towards me, he says goodbye to me by drawing a sign in the air that only he and I understand, and he smiles. His eyes are smiling, as if he knows what I read on the paper, as if he realizes that I would write his story one day…

I walk into the huge dining room which is flooded with sun rays from the skylight that makes up part of the ceiling. There are countless tables lined up next to each other, all the chairs are occupied. They sit me down at the corner of one of the tables, with the children from Angola. This is the first time I'm seeing a black person, everyone at the table is black except for me. I try to blend in, I don't want them to notice me, and I hang my head low as I feel them staring at me. One of the Angolans, realizing that I was intimidated by my new settings, picks up a piece of bread from his plate and holds it out to me, smiling. Another pours a ladle of food into my plate, gesturing for me to eat it. Everyone eats quickly, going through their second helpings, while I just stare at their hands in awe; their palms are white, everyone has palms that were as white as mine... I suddenly notice Kamil a few tables away, eating with his head bowed.

"Kamil, I've had a new dream. I dreamed about you," I say with excitement, sitting down opposite him, "My aunt's husband was waving at me from far away and there were churches with lofty domes around him. Everything was like the dreams form the previous nights, except that I did not go to the car this time, I walked toward one of the churches, and I saw you when I entered it. You were sitting in the middle of the church, on the floor; you looking at me and not noticing me. Then you suddenly started smiling. You raised your hands to your head and they had been healed. You used your fingers to open your temples, and countless birds flew out from there... The birds were rushing upward, spinning beneath the dome that was inundated with light, and the church was filled with the sounds of flapping wings. Your face began to fade away then, soon turning into a skin-colored flat surface, only your eyes remained. You looked at me but, once again, you didn't notice me. I wanted to say sorry for shouting at you, but I couldn't. My attention was focused on the birds, and more of them kept coming out of your temples..."

"My hands were healed?" he asked.

I want to reply, but I hear someone behind me,

"Grigor-*gori, gori*-Grigor..."

The Uzbek boys are chanting and pointing, the woman standing in the middle of the room calls me over, based on the paper in her hand I guess that she has read out my name. I'm going home...

"You said my hands were healed? Completely cured?" he follows me and says repeatedly.

"..."

"…"

"…"

Kamil's voice melts into my ears, and the image blurs… I'm back in my room…

I'm sitting up in bed, a dull ringing in my ears. The images have not completely been pulled out of my eyes. It is night time on the other side of the window, I try to feel my way through darkness filling the room and into the kitchen. I switch on the light, my throat is dry, I'm thirsty, there is a teapot full of water on the table. I walk up to the teapot and notice my reflection – that character is looking right back at me… I slide a finger across the nickel-lined surface and stare with curiosity, seeing the emptiness grow deeper in my eyes…

THE CITY OF DOGS

Before throwing a stone, you must ask yourself this – are you ready to intertwine your destiny with the person it hits?

I heard this story from the same Afghan boy who was always sitting near the door and looking outside. Seeing the cross hanging on my neck, he discreetly took out a small wooden one from his own pocket and showed it to me, then started telling me this story... It was so strange; if my own cross hadn't been on my neck, I would have been ready to swear that it had been mine in his hands...

I had been on the road for three days, but I had just as much to go before getting to the city. I unfurled the top of my sack but there was nothing left to eat; I emptied the breadcrumbs into my palm and, putting them into my mouth, continued to walk. I had run away from home, leaving after an argument with my father, but I can't remember why...

And so, I walked alone, in the hope that I would someday become a rich man and my father would hear about my fame. However, even in my wildest dreams, I would not have been able to imagine what fate had in store for me.

I had grown tired of walking, but the city seemed more out of reach with each step. I had never been so far from home and I had no idea what to expect in the city, I didn't even know the way there, I was relying on shepherds I met along the way and walking in the direction they indicated. It was almost dark when I noticed shadows resembling houses in the distance. Once I was convinced that the shadows were really houses, I ran excitedly, I wanted to reach the village before night had fallen completely. I thought that, once I got there, I'd come across at least one person outside, but there was nobody, to my surprise. The village was empty, deserted. "That's strange, why have they locked themselves up indoors in this heat? It's stifling," I thought, seeing the shuttered doors and windows of the houses, and kept walking.

It was completely dark by now and a full moon hung in the sky, bathing the village in a weak, milky light. I'd lost hope of seeing someone outdoors and decided to knock on the next door I came across. "Even if they don't let me stay the night, it's ok, as long as they can spare a piece of bread. I'll sleep outdoors, it won't be the first time." I knocked on a door… nobody opened. I knocked again, but there was no reply on this occasion either. But my ear caught some whispering on the other side of the door.

"I know you're home, please open the door," I shouted, knocking more loudly, "Please give me a piece of bread, I'm hungry."

I heard screams in reply, and then a deep voice said,

"Hide, it's Nasir's ghost! They must have eaten everything and left him nothing. That's why he's come home and wants to feed on our bodies!"

Scared of the strange screaming and the sound of someone crying, I ran away. I couldn't understand what had happened, all I had wanted was a piece of bread… I decided to knock on another door, but I heard screaming again, although it faded away quickly this time since there was nothing to encourage it. I walked away from that house too, and when there was terrible screeching behind the door of the third house as well, I grew convinced that none of this was a coincidence.

I was already regretting the fact that I had entered that village. I tried to remember the way I had come because I had a bad feeling and wanted to leave that place as quickly as possible. I walked in circles through the confusing paths and, for a moment, it felt like the village had grown larger. "There weren't so many houses in this place, where did they come from?" I asked myself repeatedly. Strangely enough, I had forgotten about my hunger; I felt active and energetic…

When I walked past one of the houses and was preparing to make a turn, the movement of a shadow in the distance caught my attention. I stopped to make sure that my eyes weren't playing tricks on me. The shadow was swaying, like a drunkard walking on a street. I was already scared of anything to do with that village, and a drunk person on the street was no exception. A broad-bladed knife that hung from my waist mollified my fear somewhat, I had grabbed it from home before running away. I decided to walk up to the person and ask the way out of the village; I had no other choice, I was lost. I walked towards the drunkard, trying to move my feet as quietly as possible. The closer I got, the smaller the shadow became; the moonlight was weak, and I felt like I might be seeing things. I was already quite close when several other shadows appeared next to that one, swaying in the same way… There was a bad smell and I held my breath as I tried to walk faster, when suddenly I heard a sound. I turned around automatically; the sound was coming from one of the houses that was lost in the darkness. It was growing louder and louder… I lowered my hand to the knife – I can't say what was going through my mind at that moment, the thoughts I had were quick to replace and contradict each other. At one point, I had decided to leave, but then my curiosity got the better of me; I drew a deep breath and ran to the corner from which the sound was coming. The scene that I came across was terrifying. Two shiny eyes looked out at me from the darkness, and the sound I heard was like a dog growling. Yes, it was a dog, a gigantic hound, its head lowered as it gnarled on something. It noticed me and raised its head, its shiny yellow eyes fixated on me. It all happened so quickly, all I felt was a powerful piercing sensation on my right arm, which I had raised to protect myself from an attack by the beast, while my other hand was stabbing it with the knife. The dog whined and ran away, then starting barking. My shirt was torn, I still felt a weak piercing sensation on my arm. I had not fully recovered when I heard other barking sounds mingle with the dog's, and soon there was howling coming from all sides, as if the village was surrounded by rabid dogs… "I have to find some kind of higher ground," I did not hesitate and jumped up the wall of one of the houses, trying to climb up. I somehow managed to go up, but there was a hissing in my ear and the pain in my arm was growing stronger. I ripped off my half-torn shirt to examine the extent of the injury. The dog had bitten off a piece of flesh the size of its mouth, the wound was bleeding heavily. I used the bits of my shirt to bandage it, then curled up in a corner, cringing in pain and listening to the barks alternate between sounding close up and then distant. The barking did not stop all night; it felt like the dogs were looking for me, and would not give up until they had found me. At times, I could catch sight of dogs that were running between the houses, then disappearing into the darkness…

Beneath the first rays of the morning sun, I unraveled the rags bandaging my arm. The wound was deep, but the flesh was still clinging to it – I had been mistaken when I had first examined the blood-drenched injury the previous night. I tried to stand up to see whether the dogs had gone away. My legs were finding it hard to do my bidding. Hunger and that sleepless night had drained me of strength, I barely managed to stand. I could see the village in front of me and I felt an inexplicable terror as I looked at the dusty, crooked houses. The village itself resembled a dog, it was like I could see the dog's shiny eyes in front of me… Suddenly, I heard a shout and turned my head. A thin child, covered in soot and dirt, shouted loudly, his finger pointing at me, "There he is, come over here quick, I've got him." I grew happy at first, there was hope that I would get help! But when I heard the boy shouting, I could not help feeling like I had been caught stealing something. I wanted to run away, but I stood rooted to the spot. Soon, a group of around ten people arrived, all men, and began to threaten me, saying that I should come down on my own, or they would force me down. I could not make sense of it, they kept shouting for me to come down from the roof of the house. I lowered my hand to my waist, ready for a fight, when I suddenly realized that the knife was gone, I had lost it somewhere… I had no other choice… I was a prisoner, the group did not step away from me for one minute, but they did not answer any of my questions. When I asked them to untie me because my wound had started to bleed again and it hurt, one of the men intentionally struck my arm where I was injured. We walked past the houses and I noticed people peeping out from the cracks in the windows and doorways. Many eyes were watching me, there was a sense of uncertainty and anxiety in those eyes, they were scared… Gradually, faces, heads, then whole bodies began to appear; the whole village had stepped out. Some were spitting on me, others swearing, most of the women were cursing me…

The suspense had grown unbearable. Nobody was telling me what I had done wrong, but they seemed to be taking me to be punished. The crowd kept growing larger, they were all agitated; only the grubby boy who had first spotted me skipped happily in front of everyone else. The people walking behind had already grown past three dozen, they were whispering in each other's ears… I could barely move my legs, my body felt heavy; the only thing that managed to surprise me in that situation was the large number of dogs that seemed to be everywhere. There were dogs of all kinds. The people carefully side-stepped them as they walked, while the heavy, lazy hounds did not bother to move…

The houses I could see grew fewer in number. "They're taking me out of the village," I thought. Finally, we arrived at a deserted spot, the crowd surrounded me and one of them struck at my legs from behind. My knees buckled and I fell to the floor, completely overcome with terror. The people cleared a path and a bearded old man emerged from the crowd, walking towards me at a leisurely pace.

"Is this yours?" he asked, holding out his hand.

He held my knife, which was broken. I nodded yes, and a cunning smile slid across the old man's face, as if he had been expecting that reply.

"Do you realize what you've done, you stupid boy?" he shouted, opening his green eyes wide and staring at me. The crowd was silent.

"Please, spare me," my eyes welled up.

Hearing my words, the man sprung forward and pressed the sharp end of the broken knife to my neck.

"You're a blasphemer, that's what you are! I would take the utmost pleasure in cutting your neck open with this very knife, and plucking your tongue out right here, but the rules don't allow it." He took a few steps back. "You will die a slow, torturous death; that is the right way to inflict the death sentence on blasphemers."

The words "death sentence" rung so heavy in my ears that I felt for a moment like I was underwater. When I said that there had been a mistake, that I had not committed blasphemy, the crowd made such a noise that I felt that they would attack me at any moment.

"Boy, you said the knife is yours, didn't you?" the old man asked with a smile. The smile meant that he was the only one in charge of the situation, "Weren't you the one who used it last night?"

"I did use it. A rabid dog attacked me, I stabbed the animal," I replied rapidly, confused, "But I swear that I haven't harmed anyone, that disgusting dog attacked me and all I did was…"

"You're the disgusting one, you fool! You don't understand anything! You just proved what I said. You're a blasphemer!"

I could no longer hold back, the tears began to roll down my face. I had thought that an honest confession would change the situation, but he said

that I had simply somehow confirmed my guilt, it made no sense to me…
The old man looked at me and guessed that I was dying to better understand
everything, and so he started his story. At first, I thought it had nothing to
do with me, but I soon understood what I had done wrong. He was talking
in a loud voice, without looking at me, his eyes turned to the crowd, as if
he was telling the story to the people. He talked about how, long ago, when
their forefathers had just come to those lands, they had brought with them a
tradition that was unusual, one that the other villages considered terrifying.
He talked about how, in contrast to the other villages, they did not have a
graveyard; instead, they gathered the bodies of their dead in one place, so
that the hungry dogs would eat them…

"From then on, we have been observing this tradition to this day," he said,
ending his story, "Whoever dares harm a dog is considered a blasphemer,
and must be subjected to the harshest of death sentences, because dogs are
sacred to us. Like our forefathers before us, we too believe that when a dog
eats a corpse, it absorbs the soul of the deceased. And so, our loved ones live
again, in the bodies of the dogs."

When he finished talking, I began to scream from the fear of dying. I
asked them to forgive me, I swore that I did not know that the dogs were
considered sacred, I wept and started to strike myself…

"Silence! You gained a few additional minutes of life while I was telling
this story, but enough is enough. Your time is up!"

The old man signaled to the crowd and they moved in unison, crouching
to pick up stones. It is difficult to say exactly what happened next. It was
like the events that followed all condensed into a single second… A scene
replayed from my childhood that I thought I had forgotten, and the words
that kept ringing in my head were, "I wonder what he's feeling right now?"

When I was little, my father would often take me for walks. One day,
when my father and I were walking outside, we noticed that some people
had gathered in a crowd, so we moved closer to them. A man was crouched
before them, begging to be released. He was telling them that he had a
mission, but the crowd merely laughed. My father gave me a little stone
and told me to get ready, I was going to throw it at the man. Everyone was
overjoyed when they noticed what my father had done, I had been given
the honor of casting the first stone. Seeing my father's enthusiasm excited
me, I couldn't wait to throw the stone. One of the men standing next to me,

seeing the kneeling man, said, "I wonder what he's feeling right now?" as I pulled my arm back awkwardly and released the stone. It struck the man on the chest. He looked me in the eyes, smiled, and made a strange gesture with his hand, as if drawing something in the air. The movement angered the crowd, and rocks began to rain down on him… My father took me away from there, and I learned later that the lapidated man had died. They said that he had been a Christian, going towards the grave of his God. I did not understand what Christian meant, and when I asked my father, he said that it meant he was a bad person…

These events from years before had been etched into my memory, and reappeared before me in a second. For a moment, I even felt like I could smell my father's shirt… Those words kept ringing in my head – "I wonder what he's feeling right now?" The crowd stood ready, waiting for the old man's signal. Death had never been closer…

"I feel fear," I shouted, noticing that they were preparing to throw the stones and, although my hands were tied together, I somehow managed to draw the same sign in the air that the Christian had made before he was lapidated. I closed my eyes…

"Wait!" I suddenly heard someone say.

"He's a Christian," they whispered to each other.

The old man stared as if wishing to annihilate me with his eyes. Nobody moved.

"Lower the stones," he commanded, wiping the sweat from his brow and, seeing that some of the people were not obeying his orders, he shouted,

"Whoever casts a stone on this blasphemer will then have to eat the corpse himself. I won't allow the dogs to eat a Christian."

Everything was confused in my mind; I could not understand what was happening. The old man kept shouting, "Don't commit blasphemy, respect what is sacred." Soon, everyone had dropped the stones.

"Killing you is pointless," he said, cutting the ropes that tied my hands, "You are a Christian, and so you are unclean. I cannot allow your body to be fed to our sacred animals. Go, and never show yourself in these parts again!"

The pieces of my broken knife where cast before me, and the crowd departed. Only one light-haired dog remained. It sniffed the pieces of the knife before turning around and racing after the crowd… I managed to make it to the city and stay alive, but something kept bothering me.

Years had gone by from what had been the most terrifying day of my life. I decided to go back and look again, from a distance, at the crooked houses. I wanted to understand what had been gnawing at me. But I was unable to find the village. The strangest thing was that when I asked questions about the place to an old shepherd that knew those parts very well, he said that he had never heard of that village, even though he had been herding sheep in that area since he was a little boy. I searched for that mysterious village for a long time, but in vain. I could not find a trace of it, like it had never existed at all.

THE FLY

Its head, chest and legs were covered in barely noticeable hairs, it had short whiskers, and its transparent wings looked like silver. It had frozen on the wall, as if lying in wait. Like a favorite tune, the thought kept floating in my head that it would speak to me at any moment; and it would definitely speak Armenian, it was an Armenian fly, after all.

"What are you doing?" Kamil asked.

"Looking at the fly."

"Come and draw with us, I've saved you a piece of paper."

I looked at the fly one more time, it felt so dear to me I could cry, it looked like one of the flies we had back home. I was sure that the German flies looked different, the fly on the wall was one of those we had back home… When I walked in, everyone was drawing. I picked up a piece of paper and a pencil, and settled down in a corner. I looked at the armless Georgian. We were all drawing for him, although we hadn't agreed on this in advance, and we could not have come to such an agreement, even if we had wanted to. Hayk said his name was Lasha. The men with the medical masks were taking off his shirt right there in front of us, and giving him an examination. Fear gnawed at our minds as we silently absorbed the sight of his absent arms, and none of us wanted our own arms cut off.

"How did he lose his hands?" I asked Hayk.

"I don't know."

"Haven't you asked him?"

"I have."

"And?"

"He swore at me. I'm not going to ask him again, he used a swear word with 'mother' in it…"

Kamil had drawn a dog, and he had written something next to it. All of us folded our papers in unison and placed the sheets under Lasha's pillow.

Everyone was happy except for him. There was infinite anger in his eyes, those eyes always held anger. They said that it was because he had no arms, it had made him angry at everyone. When I walked up to him, he was sitting on his bed. He looked into my eyes and then down at the untied shoelaces of his sneakers. I bent down and tied them. Nobody forced me to do so, nobody had told us to take off his shoes before bedtime and tie his laces in the morning. But all of us took care of him.

"Aren't you coming? The door is open," Kamil said.

"You go, I'll be there soon."

As I walked through the corridor, I looked at the wall, the fly was gone. Saddened by the fly's departure, I stood near the door and looked around, hoping that there would be an Armenian this time among the gathered people. The masked men had placed benches in front of the door so that nobody could approach us. The group contained children of various ethnicities – they had come to see their compatriots. Kamil said that they had been here for at least a year. Everyone had found someone from the same country – they were talking and laughing. There were girls in the group too. The pants I had been given were small in size, they clung tightly to my legs and looked awkward. I was embarrassed.

"Didn't find anyone? Nobody at all?" Kamil asked.

I didn't make a sound, I was looking at the group from the corner of my eye, convinced that everyone was looking at my pants…

"Are you Armenian?" I heard someone say.

A short boy with gray eyes was looking at me, a large, black tar-like plastic bag hanging from his shoulder.

"I knew it! I could tell as soon as I spotted you… My name is Aram. Let me get rid of this trash and I'll be right back…"

My conversation with Aram did not last very long. He got rid of the black bag and returned, we exchanged a few words, but it was enough for me. I looked at Kamil and wanted him to hear us, to strain his ears to catch our conversation but not understand a word – to listen, but not understand. Aram's voice trembled in the air, I felt like I could see the sounds he made, it was as if we were talking the loudest of all, and everyone had grown silent to listen to us. But we were speaking a secret language, one that only the two of us could understand… Our conversation seemed brief to me, he told me that he was from Goris, and it was his third year here, he asked what illness had brought me to these parts, and so on, and so forth. In the end, he said that he had completed his treatment and was going home.

"We're going back tonight. Whoever doesn't go tonight will have to stay. The next flight is going to be in a year."

When the lights went out and we got into bed, Kamil was talking. I looked at the streak of light stretching across the ceiling, the one coming from the door left ajar. I felt an explicable sense of panic, and I tried to trace it back to its cause, to understand why it was happening, but the light on the ceiling kept distracting me, it didn't let me focus. I didn't want to hear Kamil talk, I wanted him to shut up, I wanted everyone to shut up... Soon, the room submerged into silence, only the sound of the air conditioner attached to a level slightly lower than the ceiling could be heard. I was crying, my tears burning my cheeks. I couldn't forget what Aram had said, and I imagined a plane taking off without me, soaring into the sky. The scene repeated and seemed realistic. I had no doubt about it – I had lost my sense of time, and everything seemed too real and tangible to be a delusion. I could hear the sound of the plane's engines, it was the same plane that had brought us here, it would be the one to take the cured children back. The sound would fade and grow soft, as if flying away, but then would return the next second, as if this were a game, someone was having fun by watching how I was clinging on to each sliver of hope.

My mind cleared for a second, as if someone said to me, "You can't hear the sound of a plane, the airport is far away from here, remember how long the bus took to bring you to this place? Don't you remember how you'd placed your forehead against the window, watching in amazement as the endless forest slipped by? You had never seen trees like that before. All the children were crying, but you were looking out the window. You couldn't see the tops of the white trees; they were too tall. There were black spots like birthmarks on all the trees. You looked at them and held back your tears." I realized, I knew that there was no sound of a plane, that I could not possibly hear such a thing, it was the sound of the air conditioner creating that illusion, but it was no use. My consciousness soon slipped back into the subjugation of the sounds, and the air conditioner seemed to guess what was on my mind, as it slowly transformed and turned into the sound of a bus to dispel any doubts (it was more probable that I would hear a bus than a plane). I could see the bus right there, getting ready to move. Aram was sitting at the window, all the children were happy, they were all going home, except for me…

I was certain that the bus was out in the yard and I would see it if I walked to the glass door – the lights from the vehicle would betray its hiding place, they most certainly would. But when I leaped out of bed and went to the glass door, all I saw was the opaque night. I looked back and forth, unable to believe that I had missed it. "What are you doing here? Missed what? What would you have done if you hadn't missed it? The door is closed, what could you have done if you had seen the bus? What if the guard saw you now? The light is on in his room, he's watching television. What would he think if he saw you standing near the door?"

When I walked unnoticed past the half-open door of the masked man keeping watch at night, and rushed to get back to bed, an amazing thing happened. The fly was on the wall again, in the very same spot where I had last seen it. It was frozen, as if lying in wait. I kneeled in front of it. I looked at the fly and the fly looked back at me. The thought that this was a fly from home once again overcame me. I looked at it and felt certain that it would speak to me at any moment, that it would have Aram's voice… I was on my knees, crying, when I noticed that Lasha had been standing at the door, watching me. There was infinite anger in his eyes, they were always full of anger. They said that it was because he didn't have any arms, but this time it was different – his frowning eyes looked at me and showed no forgiveness. He had no arms but he did not cry, I had both of mine but was shedding tears…

All night, the sounds gave me no peace. I could hear the plane, then the bus. The sounds alternated with each other, but I no longer cried. I lay in bed, looking at the light on the ceiling, and I felt like my body was growing smaller. I had not wanted Lasha to see me crying, but it was too late, I could do nothing about it. I could do nothing about anything anymore…

When my eyes opened at the shrill sound, it was already daylight. I had felt so weak that I had not realized how long I'd slept. One of the Afghan boys had found a toy whistle and was blowing into it. The boys were bunched up near the door, making it misty with their breaths and having fun. I stood in the corner and watched, the cold morning sliding across my body. "Why is it so cold in the summer?" I was surprised. "It wasn't like this in Armenia. Kamil said that the summers weren't cold back in his country either. They're only cold here…"

"Good morning, how are you?" I heard someone ask.

Aram stood there in front of me, a large, black tar-like plastic bag hanging from his shoulder once again. Only his clothes were different.

"Aram, you're still here? I thought you said you were leaving at night," I asked, confused.

"We *are* leaving, you must have misunderstood. The plane is leaving tonight…"

"…"

"…"

"…"

He indicated what he was wearing, saying several times that only the children that were going home got new clothes. He then said that he would get a blue assistance bag, which had all kinds of items and money in it… I listened without interrupting him, but my eyes had locked on to his birthmark. There was a small birthmark beneath one of Aram's eyes. How had I not noticed it before?

"We're leaving tonight. Whoever doesn't go tonight will have to stay. The next plane is in a year," he said one more time, as if to avoid any awkwardness, and left.

Aram had long since dropped out my range of sight, but I kept standing at the glass door and looking out. I looked out of the corner of my eye at the children that had gathered, there were girls among them too. Everyone was staring at my pants, but I thought of the fly and felt sad…

STIGMA

To Sandro, who came to visit me every day, and felt sincere regret on each of those days because I was not Georgian.

Hayk used to say that death was a place with blue carpets, which issued a particular stench.

"How do you know?" I asked.

"That's how it is."

"But why blue carpets?"

"I don't know. When my father was dying, he saw blue carpets and kept wrinkling his nose, as if trying to sniff them."

"…"

"…"

"…"

I left Hayk near the door and entered the room. The boys were playing ball. His words kept spinning around in my head, reminding me of the incident in the plane. When I had just boarded the plane, they sat me down next to a Georgian boy who had curled up in his seat and fallen asleep. I didn't know he was Georgian at the time, he looked exactly like an Armenian. I was sure that he was Armenian and that this was why we had been seated next to each other. The plane had just taken off and straightened up in the sky, when something happened to the boy next to me. He started shouting in his sleep and then, with tears in his eyes, kicked at me hard. I barely managed to avoid his blows. The personnel on the plane—the doctors and other officials—gathered around the boy, but he kept shouting "Mama" and landing blows to his left and right…

"Did that scare you much?" a woman walked up to me and asked in Russian, once the boy had gone back to sleep and everything had calmed down.

"I wasn't scared," I tried to conceal my agitation.

"Really? Wow, you're a real man," she smiled, and she looked like an Armenian too. "Why are you holding your arm? Does it hurt?"

"No, no reason…"

Our conversation didn't last long. The woman said that she represented the Georgian delegation and was accompanying the Georgian children. When I asked what had happened and why the boy was calling out to his mother, she said that his father had died a few days ago, and he was probably dreaming of his funeral. The reply seemed strange to me. I could not understand why he was shouting for his mother if it had been his father who had died. Everything started to make sense once I met Hayk, an Armenian from Tbilisi. When he heard the story, he explained that the Georgians used the word "mama" to refer to their fathers. How strange!

I was lost in these thoughts when Kamil walked up to me and said,

"They've distributed the paper, you coming?"

"…"

"…"

Kamil was walking up to the boys and excitedly telling them that the sheets of paper had been distributed, we were supposed to write a letter to God. I was sure that this was another of his fibs. It wasn't the first time he was making something like this up and convincing us all it was true, before bursting with laughter at our naivety. But he hadn't been lying this time. Soon, two people with doctor's masks came in with white envelopes for the letters.

"Wait, let me think… Do the letters have to be short, or can we write long ones?" he asked, "God probably doesn't have time to read a lot of text. It has to be short; nobody reads a lot these days."

"Kamil, can one of the boys write instead of me? I'm not good at spelling in Russian, I'll make spelling mistakes."

"You're my friend, you have to write my letter instead of me."

As he was thinking long and hard about what he could write to God, I recalled the scenery that I had seen from the airplane window, something I would never forget for the rest of my life. Outside the window, it was white everywhere, as if the snow had come down and covered everything, as if this was a different world where people had not yet constructed any buildings or factories, there were no cars, pedestrians, dogs, cats; there was nothing except for a brightly-lit infinite space. I looked and thought about how good it would be if I could slip out of the plane at that moment and run around on the clouds. The other children probably wanted to do the same, many of them were on a plane for the first time, like me, and they were enchanted by the oval windows like I was, unable to look away…

"You know, Kamil? On the plane, when I was looking out the window, I saw God's throne," I said, "It was a huge chair—gigantic—made by one of the clouds. As soon as I saw it, I knew it was God's throne, but there was nobody on it…"

"…"

"…"

"…"

"Please cure my hands so that I can start riding a bicycle again." I wrote this and, cleared of my responsibility, rushed out to the corridor. I wanted to be alone when I wrote my own letter. I didn't know what to write; actually, I knew what to write, but I couldn't put my thoughts together the way I had for Kamil – I didn't know the specific purpose for which I wanted my arm to get better… I saw Hayk standing near the door, talking. The boy he was talking to looked very strange. His curls were long, like a girl's, the sun-colored strands cascading over his shoulders. He was tall, a real giant. I stood there and looked at him when he noticed me and said something to Hayk.

"This is Sandro, he's from Georgia," Hayk turned around and said to me, "He thought you were Georgian too…"

It turned out that Sandro was one of the so-called older residents. He was at least five or six years older than us and knew everything about the place. When he found out that we were writing a letter to God, he said that in the end, when one's treatment was complete and it was time to go home, everyone without exception was given a blue bag, which also contained the letters.

"Each person has their own letter placed in their bag," he said and added with a smile, "The letter returns to the person after God has read it."

"…"

"…"

"I don't believe in God," Hayk said unexpectedly, "There's no God, and that's final…"

"So what are you going to write in the letter?" I asked without thinking.

"What am I going to write? I'll write, 'Every time they switch off the light and I lie down in bed, and I see the streak of light from the half-open door slide across the ceiling, why do I always want to cry?"

"My father wouldn't have died if God really existed," he continued after a brief pause.

We didn't say anything after that. We said goodbye to Sandro and went to our beds. The lights went off…

"Someone has forgotten to flush the toilet again," Kamil said, rolling his eyes, "Must have been one of the Afghans…"

"…"

"…"

The cold morning was unusual. We were standing near the door and talking… I was taken aback when I heard a familiar voice. Sandro stood there, on the other side of the benches that had been placed so that nobody could approach us. He said something to me in Georgian.

"Good morning, Sandro. How are you? I asked, happily.

"How do you know my name?"

"…"

"…"

"…"

I was sure he was kidding, pretending to be surprised so that he could confuse me. But jokes should be in good taste, this one was boring. I had no patience for his play acting.

"I thought you were Georgian," Sandro exclaimed, then said goodbye and left.

It was strange. I could not make head or tail of it and would probably have not understood at all, if Hayk had not said,

"Sandro's head has a hole in it. It's a rare condition, he keeps having memory loss… He told me himself, he warned me that I shouldn't be surprised if he didn't remember me… No matter how much they operate on him, it's no use, the injury does not heal…"

Then he added,

"Haven't you noticed the scars on his head? The scars are big, they're covered by his hair, but you can see them if you look closely…"

Hayk continued to speak and I listened attentively, without interrupting him, as an inexplicable panic grew in my heart. I thought that, if I looked at my own arm, I would see the scars that he mentioned.

KAMIL

Ezra Pound

That part of my life was like walking in a fog. I would advance, but the fog would grow thicker. The more I walked, the mistier everything grew around me. But would you believe that now, as I try to extract the images from those difficult times from the depths of my memory, they appear before me as strangely sunny days? I cannot find an explanation for this… Despite myself, I start to believe that when the days had no end, I too had been infinite. Perhaps I truly was without end in those times…

"No, I don't like hospitals. Do you know anybody who likes them? Nobody likes them, you'd have to be an idiot to love those horrible places. But nobody can hate them as much as I do; I hate them more than anyone else in the world. Hospital corridors have a typical smell, but one that manages to brand itself into your memory despite its commonness. It's enough to step into a corridor just once—that's it!—the smell penetrates your nose. The next time you smell it, you won't be able to stop your heart from trembling no matter what you do. My mother says that it's the smell of medication, but there are all kinds of medicines in drug stores, how come they don't have the same smell?" Hayk paused for a moment, as if waiting for me to respond, but seeing that I was quiet, he continued, "No, it's not the smell of medication, that's for sure. I don't know where that smell comes from… One day, when my mother had taken me to yet another examination, an interesting thing happened. We were waiting for our turn to go to the doctor's office when the old man sitting next to me started to cry. Nobody had said anything to him, he just started sobbing for no reason. When my mother signaled the nurses to help the old man, they were not surprised and told her not to worry, this had happened before. It turned out that the old man would come to the hospital every day because he could not stay home alone, he was afraid he would die.

"…"

"…"

I left Hayk in the room and went to the corridor to drink some water. Nobody drank water from the tap there, only from plastic or glass bottles. When I had just arrived and did not yet know my way around, I needed a drink of water and naively walked up to a tap. The people with the doctor's masks got so upset that I almost died of embarrassment. I was the focus of everyone's attention, they were all explaining that tap water was only meant for washing. I wanted to say that I had not tried to do anything shameful, that everyone would drink tap water back in my country, there was nothing wrong with that. But I didn't speak German, and I could not say much in English…

"Want to see a magic trick?" Kamil approached me and asked.

"What magic trick?"

"No, first tell me if you want to see one."

"I do."

He held out the palm of his hand to me; it had a dead fly in it. He began to make faces and speak gibberish as if he was casting a magic spell, asking me to watch the fly closely. A few minutes had barely passed before the fly began to move. At first, it was as if it did not understand where it was and what was happening to it. It rolled about from one part of the palm to the other, like it was drunk. But a little while later, it gathered its strength and flew off.

"How did you do that?" I kept saying, awestruck. He laughed; he was overcome with amusement.

"…"

"…"

"…"

Kamil explained that he would catch a fly, place it in a box, and put it in the freezer of our refrigerator. After taking the box out, the fly would seem dead but, as soon as it grew slightly warmer, it would "come back to life."

"Flies are like tortoises and frogs," he explained, "I've done this trick many times back home. My family was just as surprised as you were when they first saw me do it…"

"Don't tell the other boys, I want to surprise them with the trick too," Kamil said and ran off in excitement to catch a fly.

I thought that if I had performed this trick at home it would have surely made my father mad. He wouldn't have hit me; he had never struck me once. But he would have been very angry to learn I had put the fly in the fridge, near the food. I grew sad when I thought about my father. I was sure he needed me very much and would give anything if only to have me by his side again. I didn't miss him, I didn't miss anybody or anything, except for the wallpaper we had back home. I would always dream of that wallpaper and see how I was touching its white surface, my fingers running over the pattern. There was an inexplicable sense of panic in all of it, I would wake up with tears on my cheeks, with no idea why I was crying…

I quenched my thirst and then went back into the room. Hayk and some of the boys had gathered around one of the beds. The Uzbek whom I disliked most of all—even more than two of the Afghans—and who liked me least of all, was talking about a fascinating incident.

"…when the hot air had hung low in the gorge, and when silence had risen to the sky from the scorched rocks, an amazingly beautiful snake had come out and bitten a boy. He had reached out his hand in an attempt to grab the snake by its head, but the snake had bitten him. Nobody had been down in the gorge that day except for the boy, and by the time his friends had dragged the injured boy out, his hair had turned completely white. The venom had turned his hair white, but his body had fought back, and the boy had been lucky, he had lived… Those who saw him said that before the sun set, the gypsy woman was standing on a hilltop overlooking the valley, praying with her eyes closed. In the end, when the last rays of the sun were trembling over the horizon, she took her most expensive ring off her finger and threw it off the hilltop. Her son had recovered, only his white hair remained to remind him of his ordeal…"

"The boy recovered because the gypsy woman threw her ring away?" one of the boys asked.

"Gypsy's have a tradition like that. When a family member grows sick, they cast away an expensive piece of jewelry, and the person recovers. That gypsy woman and her son now live in our city, the boy's hair is white as snow, I've seen him with my own eyes," the Uzbek added.

"..."

"..."

"..."

Everyone was asking questions enthusiastically and the Uzbek—whom I disliked most of all, and who liked me least of all—replied to them. It took me a while to notice that Kamil was in the gathered group too, he listened quietly. I had not noticed him walk up. I thought that the conversation would die down soon and he would do the trick, but he never did…

"My father used to say that scorpions are noble creatures because they know how to commit suicide, like humans do. Every time we went to gather blackberries, he would show me the herbs to use to treat a scorpion sting. He kept saying that in nature, just like in life, good and evil stand very close to each other. Wherever there were scorpions, the herbs to treat their stings could not be far, that was how nature operated… When my father was dying, pigeons had gathered on the balcony of our house. I was angry and kept scaring the off, but they would return with amazing audacity…"

When the lights went out and we went to bed, Hayk was still talking, telling us about his father. His voice grew more and more distant, his words floating in the darkness of the room. Sleep would have surely emerged victorious soon, it would have weighed down my eyelids if not for that unexpected weeping. Kamil was sitting up in bed and crying loudly. We gathered around his bed and tried to understand what had happened.

"Where does it hurt?"

"It doesn't hurt anywhere."

"So what's wrong with you?"

"If I'd known sooner about it, I would have thrown away one of my mother's jewels. I would have found something at home and cast it away," he sobbed, "I didn't know… I didn't know… What can I do now? I don't have any expensive jewelry with me…"

Kamil kept repeating those words and crying louder. We had gathered around him and tried to calm him down. The German with the doctor's mask—the one that was on duty that night—was confused, trying to understand what was going on. He asked me why the boy was crying, what had happened. I wanted to answer his question, but I didn't speak German, and I could not say much in English…

I AM AN ALARM CLOCK

The fog grew thicker. The more I walked, the mistier everything grew around me. I kept walking, looking at the stones falling under my dew-covered shoes. I was certain I had seen them before, but I could not remember where. Then I recalled that there had been stones just like these ones on the beach, when my father and I were in Batumi… I felt like I would see my father if I walked a bit further, I wanted to tell him I was sorry; I felt guilty for some reason, as if I had offended him. I had forgotten that he had died; the stones were there, and that meant that my father was somewhere close by too. But soon, I forgot everything, an unusual feeling distracted me; a fear had crept into my heart that I was lost. When I was little, my mother and I went to the store to buy me some clothes. At some point, I could no longer see my mother and I felt like I was lost. This was the same feeling I had in my dream; I was walking around in confusion, looking at the stones beneath my feet, when a shadow that came from nowhere embraced me. The thin, scrawny shadow hugged my shoulders and released them, then hugged and released again. Instead of flinching or running away, I was hitting it, striking it with all the strength I could muster, but it was in vain, and there was no need to do that. It was as if this was what it wanted me to do, as if it was mocking me…

"I could not see its face, but when I woke up, I was certain that the shadow was smiling," Hayk said, finishing his story.

"…"

"…"

"…"

I left Hayk in the room and stepped out into the corridor to drink some water. Nobody drank water from the tap there, only from plastic or glass bottles…

"If he whistles one more time, I'm going to bash his head in," Kamil said, walking up to me, "He's doing it on purpose, trying out patience. He whistles one more time and I'm bashing his head in, you'll see…"

"…"

"…"

Kamil said a couple of inappropriate words to the thin Afghan with the cracked skin like a melon peel, and then he left. I thought that the Afghan would raise his fingers to his lips again and let out a wild whistle, ruining our sleep. He was doing this for the third day in a row; as soon as day broke, he would sit up in his bed and whistle. Kamil and some of the boys had long been itching for a fight with the Afghans, they were waiting for a good excuse. I was sure that a fight would break out soon, but I couldn't be a part of it because of my arm. I couldn't avoid fighting either, what would the boys think of me?

After quenching my thirst, I went back to the room, Hayk and some of the boys had gathered around one of the beds. The Uzbek was telling them about an interesting incident.

"…classes had ended and I was going home from school, when the gypsy woman stopped me and asked how she could get to the metro station. I showed her the shortest route to the metro and was about to continue my walk home when she suddenly began to insist on rewarding me – she wouldn't let me leave without returning the favor, she wanted to tell my fortune… After a long monologue, she told me to wrap my ring in a bank note and hold it out to her. I refused, I couldn't do what she had asked, but the gypsy woman pointed to her unborn child and swore that she was not trying to trick me. She was pregnant indeed, and her promise seemed convincing. I did as she said, wrapping my ring in a bank note, and I gave it to her. She took it and blew on the money; lo and behold, my ring vanished before my very eyes… She made me promise not to tell anyone what had happened and only then let me go, assuring me that the ring would return to me, that I would find it in a fish… It wasn't a gold ring, nor was it silver, it didn't really have much value, but it was dear to me. My father had worn it on his finger for a long time, then he had given it to me… Such a thing had never happened to me before, I didn't know what to do; what was I supposed to say at home, where was my ring? I would go home, and my father would not notice it, but my mother would immediately see that it wasn't on my finger… So, I walked with tears in my eyes and people passed by next to me. A woman stopped and started asking questions, trying to figure out what had happened to upset me, but I slipped past her – the gypsy had warned me not to tell anyone, hadn't she? She had said that the ring would not come back if I told anyone. I had walked past several streets when I heard a voice behind me – it was the gypsy woman, she was running toward me. She caught up to me and breathlessly put the ring in my hand, then ran away…"

"…"

"…"

"…"

Everyone started asking questions enthusiastically, and the Uzbek answered them all. I did not want to hear any more and was about to leave when Kamil came up to me with a smile on his face.

"Do you have a navel-cotton-stuffer?"

"What?"

"A navel-cotton-stuffer. It's a small, purple creature that secretly stuffs cotton fluff into people's belly buttons," and he could not resist laughing, then added, "I made it up. What do you think?"

"It's good. But why purple?"

"I don't know, it's my favorite color…"

"…"

"…"

When the lights went out and we went to bed, Kamil was still talking, swearing at the Afghan. His voice grew more and more distant, his words floating in the darkness of the room. Sleep soon emerged victorious, weighing my eyelids closed…

"Nobody tricked you, right? All right, then. Drop the cat in the water," said Karen, whom the children in the yard liked least of all, and who disliked me the most. "Let's see it walk on water."

Narek didn't make a sound, he stared back and blinked.

"Can't you hear me? Are you deaf? I said, drop it in the water…"

The backpack floated on the silvery surface, bobbing up and down as if trying to grab hold of a rock. But the water flowed quickly, very quickly. For a moment, Narek stood immobile, watching the departing backpack as if hypnotized, doing nothing. Perhaps he couldn't believe that he no longer had it, that his fingers had handed them over so easily to someone else, with no resistance. He knew, he had felt that there had been resistance, his fingers had not given up quickly; they hurt now, there was a prickly feeling in his palm, but he was doing nothing… Perhaps he understood well what was going on, perhaps he was simply waiting for something to happen, watching and waiting… When the backpack was already at such a distance that it looked like just a yellow dot, he regained his senses, as if the fog that had been gathering around him had suddenly disappeared, and it was only then I realized that Narek's face looked like mine, it was me…

When the dream had been plucked from my eyes, there was a ruckus in the room. The Afghan was whistling, pushing out all the air his lungs could hold; the sharp, piercing sound cut through the semi-darkness of the room and poured into our ears. Everything happened quickly after that. Kamil moved like an agile creature that had been lying in wait for its prey all night. He leaped out of bed, sped towards the Afghan and I was certain a fight was going to break out. But he returned soon.

"He said that he's an alarm clock. He claims that he's the only thing that is keeping us from being prisoners of our dreams," he laughed, holding his stomach, as he repeated what the Afghan with the cracked skin like a melon peel had said.

Kamil repeated what the Afghan had said several more times, and the boys cracked up laughing, their eyes getting teary. Everyone was happy, except Hayk and me.

GUARDS

So, on that day, I was standing at the window and looking out, unable to hold back my smile. My attention was focused on an amusing scene – right beneath my window, a small box had been placed on the curb, a pair of partially worn out shoes next to it. The image was completed by a piece of cardboard resting against the box that said, "Help the Invisible Man." I thought to myself, I wonder who came up with this idea? It was a good one – why stand in the cold and freeze or catch a kidney infection when you can beg for money this way?

I put on my coat and the warmest cap I could find, then I stepped outside for a walk. I was still thinking about the Invisible Man, it was amusing indeed. I recalled the beggars I would see every day – the old man who walked around the Opera, beseeching people in a hoarse voice, "Help me with something, anything!" Or the Russian-speaking woman who was begging money for surgery for a disabled person. I also recalled the boy with the ball who performed football tricks on Freedom Square to entertain people. It's like he's in charge of the city – he can sing out loud if he wants to, and when he grows tired, he can take a nap on a public bench of his choosing. He can do what he likes. I thought that I should tell them about the latest ways to beg for money, the poor things, they're working too hard at this…

I walked in the park for a couple of hours, watching a mother crow dunk a dry piece of bread in a puddle, softening it before she took it to her chick. It was fascinating – were they really that smart? I thought about various things after that, summing up the year in my head, trying to figure out whether it had been a year of gains or losses. It was already growing darker and colder, snowflake-like specks were appearing in the sky – it was time to return home. I decided to take a shortcut in order to save time, so I ducked into the yard of one of the buildings, and there I ended up becoming part of a strange story.

"Help me young man!" A man of sixty years was leaning against a door, seemingly unable to move.

"Are you feeling ill? Should I call an ambulance?" I said, and started walking toward him before he stopped me with a gesture.

"No need. But don't leave, all right? Don't go anywhere!"

"I won't, but what's wrong? It would be best to call an ambulance, just in case."

"I don't need anything, I'm going to die any minute now, and you need to take my place."

"…"

"…"

"…"

He was saying incomprehensible things. He said that he had been standing at that door his whole life, keeping guard so that nobody would step out. The thick lenses of his glasses had grown watery, he was crying and begging me not to leave.

"You see? He can sense that my strength is draining, he wants to come out," and he shook the door as he said this, as if there was someone behind it. "Don't go. I'm going to die any minute now, you have to take guard, so that he doesn't get out…"

There was no doubt that the man had psychiatric issues; would a normal person say things like that? I had to get out of there as quickly as possible, this wasn't the first madman I had come across on the streets. I had already made the biggest mistake by engaging in conversation with him. The right thing is not to talk to crazy people, every word you say can encourage them further and blur the boundaries between you. Your own words become your enemies, knives that are thrown toward you… I decided to leave and had barely taken a couple of steps when he fell over like a tree that had been chopped down. I could not resist, I walked up to help him but it was too late, he was dead. Upset, I ran away. I kept running, it was snowing heavily now and the large flakes dropped into my eyes, trying to make me stray from my path home. But I was running with all the strength my legs could muster, throwing myself forward, I wanted to get home as quickly as possible…

When I walked in, my clothes had stuck to my body, I was drenched from head to toe. I walked towards the bathroom, trying to get rid of the thoughts weighing on my mind and it was only then I noticed the knob of the bedroom door moving. I leaped towards the door and slammed it shut…

And although I was certain that I was alone, that there was nobody behind that door—there couldn't be, it was an absurd fear, nothing else—I remained standing in front of the door nevertheless. Night had fallen on the other side of the window, the snowflakes slowly swayed in the air and a sudden desire that had appeared in my heart grew stronger and stronger. I wanted to walk up to the window and take another look at the Invisible Man.

A Brown Man in Russia
Lessons Learned on the Trans-Siberian
by Vijay Menon

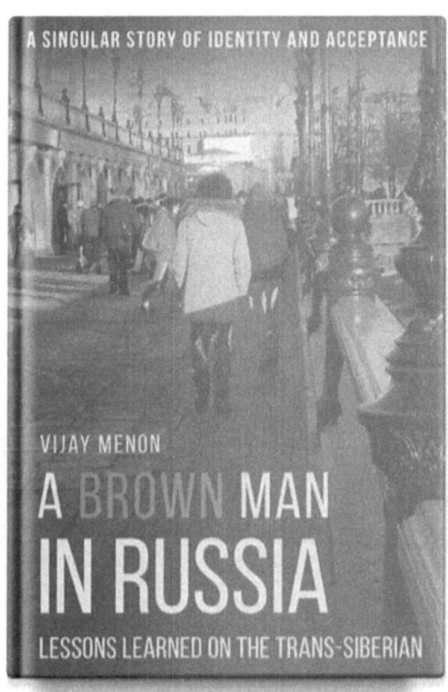

A Brown Man in Russia describes the fantastical travels of a young, colored American traveler as he backpacks across Russia in the middle of winter via the Trans-Siberian. The book is a hybrid between the curmudgeonly travelogues of Paul Theroux and the philosophical works of Robert Pirsig. Styled in the vein of Hofstadter, the author lays out a series of absurd, but true stories followed by a deeper rumination on what they mean and why they matter. Each chapter presents a vivid anecdote from the perspective of the fumbling traveler and concludes with a deeper lesson to be gleaned. For those who recognize the discordant nature of our world in a time ripe for demagoguery and for those who want to make it better, the book is an all too welcome antidote. It explores the current global climate of despair over differences and outputs a very different message – one of hope and shared understanding. At times surreal, at times inappropriate, at times hilarious, and at times deeply human, A Brown Man in Russia is a reminder to those who feel marginalized, hopeless, or endlessly divided that harmony is achievable even in the most unlikely of places.

Buy it > www.glagoslav.com

Little Zinnobers
by Elena Chizhova

Is it possible to cultivate fundamental human values if you live in a totalitarian state? A teacher who instigates the school theatre sets out to prove that it is. But while the pupils rehearse Shakespeare's tragedies and comedies under her ever-vigilant eye, Soviet life makes its brutal adjustments. This can be called a book about love, the tough kind of love that gets you through life, and death.

Zinnobers is especially fascinating for British readers as we see Shakespeare's famous sonnets and plays are touchingly brought to life by the Russian children and their gifted teacher, the novel's heroine. The teacher applies some of the playwright's satire to the socio-political situation of the USSR, using her English lessons to teach her students life's broader lessons, too.

Echoes of the Soviet Union can be felt in our own society today: the people find themselves increasingly at odds with the politicians' hypocrisy, 'big brother' is watching us through thousands of CCTVs, and political correctness determines what we can and cannot say...

Buy it > www.glagoslav.com

Leo Tolstoy – Flight from Paradise

by Pavel Basinsky

Over a hundred years ago, something truly outrageous occurred at Yasnaya Polyana. Count Leo Tolstoy, a famous author aged eighty-two at the time, took off, destination unknown. Since then, the circumstances surrounding the writer's whereabouts during his final days and his eventual death have given rise to many myths and legends. In this book, popular Russian writer and reporter Pavel Basinsky delves into the archives and presents his interpretation of the situation prior to Leo Tolstoy's mysterious disappearance. Basinsky follows Leo Tolstoy throughout his life, right up to his final moments. Reconstructing the story from historical documents, he creates a visionary account of the events that led to the Tolstoys' family drama.

Flight from Paradise will be of particular interest to international researchers studying Leo Tolstoy's life and works, and is highly recommended to a broader audience worldwide.

Buy it > www.glagoslav.com

Girls, be Good

by Bojan Babić

"Girls, be good" is an omnibus novel that consists of twenty short stories connected by a single framing narrative: just after the fall of the Berlin wall, foreign investors feel good about the investment climate in Eastern Europe and decide to open a huge toy factory in ex-Yugoslavia, where they are going to produce a hit range of toys designed for girls: small, plush lemurs called Aya, that will be sold all over the world. Before long, though, their optimism starts to feel out of place - the war in Yugoslavia begins, and the factory, having only produced one edition of the toys, has to shut down production...

Death of the Snake Catcher

by Ak Welsapar

This book features people from one of the most closed countries of today's world, where the passage of time resembles the passage of a caravan through the waterless desert. This world has been recreated by a true-born son of that mysterious country, a Turkmen who, at the will of fate, has now been living for a quarter of a century in snowy Scandinavia. Is that not why two different worlds come together in *Ryazan horseradish and Tula gingerbread*, to come apart in *Love in Lilac*, in which a student from the non-free world falls in love with a girl from the West?

In the story *Death of the Snake Catcher*, an old snake catcher meets one on one with a giant cobra in the heart of the desert. In the dialogue between them the author unveils the age-old interdependence of Man and untamed nature, where the fear and mistrust of the strong and the hopes and apprehensions of the weak change places but co-exist as ever. *Egyptian night of fear*, in which a boy goes to an Eastern bazaar and falls into the clutches of depraved forces, is created in the writer's characteristic style of magical realism, while the novella Altynai celebrates first love, radiant and sad, pure as virgin snow.

Buy it > www.glagoslav.com

Marina Tsvetaeva - The Essential Poetry

by Marina Tsvetaeva

Marina Tsvetaeva: The Essential Poetry includes translations by Michael M. Naydan and Slava I. Yastremski of lyric poetry from all of the great Modernist Russian poet Marina Tsvetaeva's published collections and from all periods of her life. It also includes a translation of two of Tsvetaeva's masterpieces in the genre of the long poem, "Poem of the End" and "Poem of the Mountain." The collection strives to present the best of Tsvetaeva's poetry in a single small volume and to provide a representative overview of Tsvetaeva's high art and the development of different poetic styles over the course of her creative lifetime. Also included in this volume are a guest introduction by eminent American poet Tess Gallagher, a translator's introduction and extensive endnotes.

Glagoslav Publications Catalogue

- *The Time of Women* by Elena Chizhova
- *Andrei Tarkovsky: The Collector of Dreams*
  by Layla Alexander-Garrett
- *Andrei Tarkovsky - A Life on the Cross* by Lyudmila Boyadzhieva
- *Sin* by Zakhar Prilepin
- *Hardly Ever Otherwise* by Maria Matios
- *Khatyn* by Ales Adamovich
- *The Lost Button* by Irene Rozdobudko
- *Christened with Crosses* by Eduard Kochergin
- *The Vital Needs of the Dead* by Igor Sakhnovsky
- *The Sarabande of Sara's Band* by Larysa Denysenko
- *A Poet and Bin Laden* by Hamid Ismailov
- *Watching The Russians (Dutch Edition)* by Maria Konyukova
- *Kobzar* by Taras Shevchenko
- *The Stone Bridge* by Alexander Terekhov
- *Moryak* by Lee Mandel
- *King Stakh's Wild Hunt* by Uladzimir Karatkevich
- *The Hawks of Peace* by Dmitry Rogozin
- *Harlequin's Costume* by Leonid Yuzefovich
- *Depeche Mode* by Serhii Zhadan
- *The Grand Slam and other stories (Dutch Edition)*
  by Leonid Andreev
- *METRO 2033 (Dutch Edition)* by Dmitry Glukhovsky
- *METRO 2034 (Dutch Edition)* by Dmitry Glukhovsky
- *A Russian Story* by Eugenia Kononenko
- *Herstories, An Anthology of New Ukrainian Women Prose Writers*
- *The Battle of the Sexes Russian Style* by Nadezhda Ptushkina
- *A Book Without Photographs* by Sergey Shargunov
- *Down Among The Fishes* by Natalka Babina
- *disUNITY* by Anatoly Kudryavitsky
- *Sankya* by Zakhar Prilepin
- *Wolf Messing* by Tatiana Lungin
- *Good Stalin* by Victor Erofeyev
- *Solar Plexus* by Rustam Ibragimbekov

- *Don't Call me a Victim!* by Dina Yafasova
- *Poetin (Dutch Edition)* by Chris Hutchins
  and Alexander Korobko
- *A History of Belarus* by Lubov Bazan
- *Children's Fashion of the Russian Empire* by Alexander Vasiliev
- *Empire of Corruption - The Russian National Pastime* by Vladimir
  Soloviev
- *Heroes of the 90s - People and Money. The Modern History
  of Russian Capitalism*
- *Fifty Highlights from the Russian Literature (Dutch Edition)* by
  Maarten Tengbergen
- *Bajesvolk (Dutch Edition)* by Mikhail Khodorkovsky
- *Tsarina Alexandra's Diary (Dutch Edition)*
- *Myths about Russia* by Vladimir Medinskiy
- *Boris Yeltsin - The Decade that Shook the World* by Boris Minaev
- *A Man Of Change - A study of the political life
  of Boris Yeltsin*
- *Sberbank - The Rebirth of Russia's Financial Giant*
  by Evgeny Karasyuk
- *To Get Ukraine* by Oleksandr Shyshko
- *Asystole* by Oleg Pavlov
- *Gnedich* by Maria Rybakova
- *Marina Tsvetaeva - The Essential Poetry*
- *Multiple Personalities* by Tatyana Shcherbina
- *The Investigator* by Margarita Khemlin
- *The Exile* by Zinaida Tulub
- *Leo Tolstoy – Flight from paradise* by Pavel Basinsky
- *Moscow in the 1930* by Natalia Gromova
- *Laurus (Dutch edition)* by Evgenij Vodolazkin
- *Prisoner* by Anna Nemzer
- *The Crime of Chernobyl - The Nuclear Goulag*
  by Wladimir Tchertkoff
- *Alpine Ballad* by Vasil Bykau
- *The Complete Correspondence of Hryhory Skovoroda*
- *The Tale of Aypi* by Ak Welsapar
- *Selected Poems* by Lydia Grigorieva
- *The Fantastic Worlds of Yuri Vynnychuk*

- *The Garden of Divine Songs and Collected Poetry of Hryhory Skovoroda*
- *Adventures in the Slavic Kitchen: A Book of Essays with Recipes*
- *Seven Signs of the Lion* by Michael M. Naydan
- *Forefathers' Eve* by Adam Mickiewicz
- *One-Two* by Igor Eliseev
- *Girls, be Good* by Bojan Babić
- *Time of the Octopus* by Anatoly Kucherena
- *The Grand Harmony* by Bohdan Ihor Antonych
- *The Selected Lyric Poetry Of Maksym Rylsky*
- *The Shining Light* by Galymkair Mutanov
- *The Frontier: 28 Contemporary Ukrainian Poets - An Anthology*
- *Acropolis - The Wawel Plays* by Stanisław Wyspiański
- *Contours of the City* by Attyla Mohylny
- *Conversations Before Silence: The Selected Poetry of Oles Ilchenko*
- *The Secret History of my Sojourn in Russia* by Jaroslav Hašek
- *Mirror Sand - An Anthology of Russian Short Poems in English Translation* (A Bilingual Edition)
- *Maybe We're Leaving* by Jan Balaban
- *Death of the Snake Catcher* by Ak WelsaparRichard Govett
- *A Brown Man in Russia - Perambulations Through A Siberian Winter* by Vijay Menon
- *Hard Times* by Ostap Vyshnia
- *The Flying Dutchman* by Anatoly Kudryavitsky
- *Nikolai Gumilev's Africa* by Nikolai Gumilev
- *Combustions* by Srđan Srdić
- *The Sonnets* by Adam Mickiewicz
- *Dramatic Works* by Zygmunt Krasiński
- *Four Plays* by Juliusz Słowacki
- *Little Zinnobers* by Elena Chizhova
- *A Flame Out at Sea* by Dmitry Novikov
- *We Are Building Capitalism! Moscow in Transition 1992-1997*
- *The Hemingway Game* by Evgeny Grishkovets
- *The Nuremberg Trials* by Alexander Zvyagintsev
- *I Want a Baby and Other Plays* by Sergei Tretyakov
- *Biography of Sergei Prokofiev* by Igor Vishnevetsky
- *Duel* by Borys Antonenko-Davydovych
- *Mikhail Bulgakov: The Life and Times* by Marietta Chudakova

More coming soon...